MW01254573

Dear Patty,
Love lives on!
All the best . . .
C.K. May
XOXO

www.ckgbooks.com

EYE OF THE STORM

C.K. GRAY

INFINITY
PUBLISHING

Copyright © 2010 by C.K. Gray

ISBN 0-7414-6018-1

Printed in the United States of America

Published August 2011

INFINITY PUBLISHING
1094 New DeHaven Street, Suite 100
West Conshohocken, PA 19428-2713
Toll-free (877) BUY BOOK
Local Phone (610) 941-9999
Fax (610) 941-9959
Info@buybooksontheweb.com
www.buybooksontheweb.com

ONE

Savannah, Georgia, 1902

More than anything in the world, Eliza loved the sunshine. She loved the way it warmed her long, sandy-blonde hair as she strolled reluctantly to school in the morning and the way it greeted her in the afternoon like an old friend who couldn't wait to see her, enveloping her in comfort after a long, boring day spent indoors. She loved the way the sun showed her the world, illuminating the leaves on the trees that lined the streets to her home and the old, familiar faces she encountered along the way—Mr. Macallister, the barber her father visited for a shave once a week, Mrs. Sloan, the seamstress who had sewn all of Eliza's dresses since she was a little girl, even old Widow Flanagan, who seemed to do nothing but sit out on her rocking chair on the front porch of her enormous house and scowl at people.

"Afternoon, Mrs. Flanagan," Eliza called, waving at the widow as she passed. The old woman weakly raised a hand in response and glowered at Eliza as she continued down the street.

On this Tuesday afternoon in early June, Eliza had just been let out of school for the day—thankfully, because she couldn't have taken another minute of it. Bright though she was—she always earned the highest marks in her class—she just couldn't stand being cooped up in the tiny, one-room schoolhouse all day, listening to Miss Wood drone on and on about one thing or another. The only time the teacher ever stopped talking was when she had to reprimand Eliza for staring out the window instead of paying attention. But Eliza couldn't help it. How could she be expected to do schoolwork when there was this whole great, big, sunshine-filled world out here just calling to her?

Something great is waiting for me in this sunshine, I can feel it, she thought as she neared the center of town, headed for the shops. That morning, her mother had given her a list of goods to order from the local mercantile after school—some soap, some sugar and various other household necessities that didn't interest Eliza in the least. Though her elders often told her she was mature for her age, at seventeen, she had not yet developed a mind for the minutiae of everyday life. She was more concerned with spending time with her friends, reading good books, discovering new things and…

She sighed. If there was one overwhelming thing that the sunshine reminded her of, it was that she didn't have anyone to share it with. All of her girlfriends had already paired off with young men who showed a great deal of promise. Mary's beau, the son of a prominent local businessman, would soon be taking over the family's feed store, which was awfully successful. Clara's young suitor, Alexander, had plans to study medicine and become a doctor.

But Eliza… Well, a couple of boys from school had shown interest in her. One had asked to walk her home one day, and another had invited her to go boating on the lake. But she had denied them both. It wasn't that they weren't sweet or handsome, but they just weren't—

"They weren't like *him*," she said quietly, coming to an abrupt halt outside the fence of the local lumberyard. Inside, a crew of men worked diligently, turning enormous tree trunks into piles of stove-sized logs. Their tanned faces covered with sawdust and sweat, they joked and shouted at one another as they worked, chiding each other into cutting and stacking the logs faster and faster. In the middle of the group, while everyone else bent over their work, one young man stood tall, pausing to push a lock of hair out of his eyes. Brown but streaked lighter by the sun, his hair was straight, a little unruly, a mess made only worse by his thick, dirty work gloves as he pawed it back into place.

Who is he? Eliza wondered, an unbidden smile sneaking onto her lips. She'd passed by the lumber mill hundreds of times before but had never seen this young man here—though, of course, being a prim and proper young lady, she had never stopped to ogle the men working there before, either. Had he been there all along, right under her nose, without her even knowing it?

How could I not have seen him? she thought now, unable to take her eyes off of him. He was surely handsome, with a muscular build and the rugged features of a man unafraid of hard work. Once his hair was out of his eyes, he resumed tossing logs onto a pile and Eliza couldn't help but notice his finely muscled arms moving easily under his white, sleeveless shirt. Tall and slim, he moved with grace, speed and obvious agility.

Yet, there was more to him than that. Eliza could not put her finger on it, but something rooted her to the spot, compelled her to follow every swing of his arm, every turn of his head. It wasn't just his looks. There was something about him, something that made her think—

"Oh!" Eliza cried out, whirling around to face the street again. Deep within her reverie, she hadn't noticed that the young man had paused again while waiting for his coworkers to cut more logs for him, nor that he had looked over at her quizzically. Wiping the sweat from his brow with the back of his forearm, he'd peered directly into Eliza's green eyes for just a second before she'd turned herself away from him, her pale cheeks blushing a rosy pink.

Putting a hand up to her warm forehead, Eliza let out a long breath and looked around her, hoping that no one had seen her staring at the man. *Get a hold of yourself, old girl,* she told herself, fighting the urge to turn back and look at him again. And before she could change her mind about it, she picked up the hem of her long skirt and ran off down the street toward the general store.

***

"Miss Anceaux," said Mr. Jackson, the owner of the mercantile shop and an old friend of Eliza's family. "What can I get for you today? Or, rather, what can I get for *your mother* today?"

"Good afternoon, Mr. Jackson," Eliza said with a smile. "Just a few things…" She handed over the list her mother had given her and he looked at it, then nodded his head.

"No problem, my dear, we have all of this in stock. I'll get it all ready for you. Won't be but a few minutes."

"Thank you," Eliza told him, then wandered off to look around the store while he prepared her order.

A trip to the mercantile was indeed a chore for Eliza, something that she wished her mother would do herself or send one of Eliza's younger siblings to do. Knowing how much she disliked it, however, her mother softened the blow a little by giving Eliza some extra change with which to purchase something for herself—a small amount of perfume, a ribbon for her hair or some candy, which she invariably shared with her brothers and sisters. Today, she had in mind the latter—some licorice, perhaps, one of her favorites. She headed over toward the candy shelf as Mr. Jackson packed up a bag for her behind the counter.

As she perused the selection of sweets, she heard the bell over the shop's front door jingle, signaling that another customer had come in. Not looking up from the candy, she heard heavy footsteps cross the store's creaky, wooden floorboards, and then a deep, strong voice began to speak.

"Afternoon, Mr. Jackson," it said. "How are you this fine day?"

"Oh, just about right as rain, John, thank you for asking. And yourself?" Mr. Jackson replied.

The man let out a low whistle. "Hot as Hades, sir. Can't wait to get down to the lake and cool off in the water!"

"Well, what can I help you with then, so you can get on your way?"

The man laughed. "I have a taste for something sweet today. I was thinking about…some *licorice*. Do you have any?"

Eliza laughed a little at the request, thinking it odd that someone had come in for just the same thing she'd decided she wanted. Still lingering by the candy shelf, she peeked out around a display of fabrics and sewing notions to see who it was who shared her sweet tooth and—

She gasped, then threw a hand over her mouth to quiet herself. She could barely believe it, but there, standing just a few feet away from her, was the young man from the lumberyard! He had a long-sleeved shirt on now, and he appeared slightly cleaner, especially about the face. But he was still tall, handsome and alluring in a way that Eliza could not explain.

"I'll tell you what, John," Mr. Jackson went on, his voice quiet and conspiratorial. Eliza saw him reach down behind his counter and pull up a small, brown-paper bag folded over at the top. "I just got in a new shipment of licorice whips. I haven't even put them out yet. They're nice and fresh. I think I can spare a few for one of my best customers."

From her hiding place, Eliza could see the man—John, she'd heard Mr. Jackson say—in profile, and his smile suddenly lit up the room. "Why, that would be fantastic," he said to Mr. Jackson, retrieving a few coins from his pants pocket and handing them over. "Thank you kindly, sir."

The two men shook hands and then John turned to go, opening the bag and reaching in for a piece of candy before he even reached the door.

"Enjoy your swim, now," Mr. Jackson called after him, and John raised his hand in a wave just before the door's bell rang again and he was gone.

Now, if I didn't know any better, Eliza thought, standing up straight again and smoothing out her skirt, *I'd say this was a sign.* Seeing John in the lumberyard and then again in the store, his sudden taste for licorice, just like hers—it couldn't have been mere coincidence. Eliza's mother was always scolding her for daydreaming, but she knew, this time, that her fantasy was real. It had to be; the signs were just too clear. There was no mistake that she had to meet this John—but how and when would be a problem.

Or would it?

The lake, she thought, a devilish smile twisting across her lips.

"Mr. Jackson," she cried, running back over to his counter, startling the poor old man half to death. "Mr. Jackson, please hurry. I suddenly have something very important to attend to!"

Two

The lake to which Eliza's mystery man had referred in Mr. Jackson's store wasn't actually a lake but a river basin, a pool of placid, cool water that eventually trickled out into a tributary and on to the great Savannah River. There were probably dozens of such areas in Georgia, these great watersheds surrounded by woods and tall grasses, the perfect gathering spots for all manner of animals—both fauna and human alike.

But Eliza couldn't imagine that those other places were anything like *her* lake, the river basin that lay just outside the city limits. When the weather was good, it was the place to be for all of Savannah's denizens, from babies in baskets to the elderly in their wheeled chairs and lap blankets, their nurses pushing them out for some much-needed sun. On warm days, the lake's water was refreshingly chilly, and Eliza and her friends had spent many carefree afternoons ensconced up to their shoulders, splashing each other and laughing until their bellies ached. On cool days, they simply brought some blankets and a picnic lunch and enjoyed the scenery, the open sky and the fresh air, with all the other escapees from the city.

Today, since it was only June and school was not yet through for the year, the lake crowd was not at full capacity, but it was definitely busy for late afternoon on a weekday. Several nannies met up near the trees with their children, who crawled around on the blankets they'd laid on the ground. In the grass, a passel of teenage boys ran after one another in some makeshift game of tag, and a few couples wandered arm in arm around the water's edge, their eyes only on each other, the world around them vanished.

Eliza smiled at this sight but felt a slight tug on her heart at the same time. She was happy for those young lovers, but they also served as painful reminders that she had no one by her side—no one to stroll with, no one to peer deep into her eyes or to whisper sweet secrets in her ear. No one with whom to share this beautiful day, with all its blue skies and sunshine, that glorious sunshine.

But then she remembered why she was there, and thought that maybe that situation was about to change.

"John," Eliza intoned to herself in a low voice, her eyes roving over the figures scattered around the lake, searching for that handsome profile, the tousled hair, the strong arms and broad shoulders that had hoisted the wood at the lumberyard so easily.

Not seeing him, she sighed, her own shoulders slumping. "John," she repeated, though this time it did not sound as hopeful. Maybe he'd decided not to come to the lake after all. Maybe he'd been delayed somewhere else—at home, perhaps, with his mother or his sister or his *wife*. What if that were the case? What would Eliza do then?

With crowds of people around her, she felt just as alone as ever and even looking up into the blue sky and squinting at her beloved sun could not change her mood. Finding the stump of a large, old tree nearby, she sat down on it forlornly to contemplate the situation. She'd been so giddy about following this strange man to the lake, so intent on finding him, that she hadn't stopped to consider that perhaps she was being ridiculous. Perhaps her mother was right—her head *was* in the clouds, even on a clear day such as this, and she needed to come back down. School would be ending soon, and not just for the summer but for good, and there were so many other things about which Eliza should be worrying. This boy, well, he really meant nothing at—

"Come on, John!" someone called from the adjacent shore, and Eliza stood up like a soldier springing to attention. Angling up onto her toes to see as far as she could, she followed with her eyes the sound of the voice, settling on the boatyard—well, it was just an area, really, where a few rows of rickety old rowboats lay, waiting for someone to take a chance on their seaworthiness. Nearby, a few young men stood, looking unbearably warm in their brown-tweed Norfolk jackets. Facing the water, they cupped their hands around their mouths and hollered to a couple of boats already out in the basin.

"Keep up, Michael, keep up!" another one of them shouted, and Eliza switched her view out to the water, to the boats at which their catcalls were directed. Each was rowed by a young man, both with their shirtsleeves rolled up to their elbows. One wore a light-colored straw boater hat but the other was bare-headed, his straight, brown hair tossing as his body moved rhythmically, his strong arms rowing and rowing, propelling his vessel across the open water at breakneck speed. That was her John, she was sure of it. She'd never felt so sure of anything in her life.

"Yes, come on, John!" she cheered along quietly, unable to take her eyes off the race. Though the other gentleman pulled his boat ahead for a moment, it was clear that John would win in the end; under his command, his dilapidated rowboat moved with the grace of a silvery minnow, slipping its way through the water with barely a ripple. Before long, he was dipping his oars low beneath the surface, dragging the craft to a slow stop as he neared the shore, his competitor left far behind, their brethren on land shouting their approval.

"Nice going, John!" one of them said, clapping him on the back with one hand and grabbing the stern of the boat with the other, pulling it up onto the ground. Without even waiting for it to stop, John hopped up and out of the boat, landing lightly on the soft earth and shaking the sweat from his hair. With his face turned up to the sunlight, Eliza could see his satisfied smile, could sense his self-assuredness; he had known all along that he would win, he'd been absolutely sure of it.

This made Eliza smile, too. Of all the things she found attractive about this man, his confidence was one of the strongest. Unlike so many of the young boys at school who seemed afraid to approach her at all, as though she would bite them if given the chance, she was sure that if he had the opportunity, John would make no bones about wanting to speak with her. He would be straightforward, honest and open with her—but courtly, of course, as any real man should be. He would be kind and caring but strong and authoritative when he needed to be, to shield Eliza from harm. And when they were alone, he would show her the most tender affection.

These thoughts hit her like a revelation, forcing her eyes to open wide as she watched John and his young friends helping the second boater onto the lakeshore. She may not have known John, not yet, but somehow she knew that all these things were true about him—that he *was* kind, he *was* caring, and that he would respect her and protect her at any cost. Just as she knew that the grass beneath her feet was green and the smoldering sun burned a hot yellow in the sky, she knew that John was everything she wanted—and that he would feel the same way about her. She could feel this with every sense her body possessed.

The only thing left to do, then, was meet him. Their fate, it seemed, lay directly in Eliza's very eager hands.

Noting that the group down by the boatyard appeared to be packing up for the day, she quickly made up her own plan in her mind and jumped into the middle of a crowd of newcomers, a group of city folk making their way down the path toward the water. Obviously unaccustomed to all that nature had to offer, they moved slowly, the women grasping their skirts with clenched fists and peering down at their pointed boots, wary of the somewhat soggy marshland beneath them. The men, though they offered their arms for support, did not seem much more comfortable with the situation themselves. Their eyes scanned the water and the tree line as if on guard against a sudden influx of angry wildlife.

From behind this motley clan, Eliza peeked out to see that John was indeed done with his rowing for the day and was rolling his sleeves back down as he chatted and laughed with his friends. How at ease he looked, how satisfied not just with himself but with his mates around him. These must have been his good friends, Eliza surmised, noting how freely they carried on with one another. She also saw how all the rest of them seemed to look up to John, standing around him in a circle as if he were their ringleader, as if they waited for him to call the shots.

As Eliza's newfound family neared the water's edge, they slowed down even further and she felt a knot growing in the pit of her stomach; now she was only feet away from John, who was shaking hands with his comrades and bidding them all a good evening. A couple of them near-begged him to stay, but he graciously backed out of the group, telling them that he had a family obligation and could stay no longer. Again Eliza wondered whom he was going home to, but she pushed that thought out of her mind, knowing that the chance she'd been waiting for was almost upon her.

"Excuse me, excuse me," she said to an awfully delicate-looking young woman accompanied by a grandfatherly gentleman. Both of them looked startled, as if Eliza were some forest creature they'd never seen before. Mutely, they paused and let her pass by them, then they returned their attention to their puzzling parade down to the waterfront.

Standing alone suddenly, between John's group and her own, Eliza stopped short, her heart in her throat.

Don't give up now, she told herself.

Swallowing hard, she bowed her head down and watched her feet as she strode directly toward John and his friends. Though to all outward appearances, she seemed lost in her own little world, she was listening to every word they said and monitoring their moves out of the corner of her eye. As she approached them, an ever-so-subtle change in her tack brought her closer to them than ever, so close that she could smell the scent of John's cologne, a rich, musky scent that instantly inebriated her. She closed her eyes and drew in a deep breath...and tripped on her own feet, landing squarely against John's side and startling him immensely.

"Whoa, whoa!" he cried, grabbing on to her arms tightly, his large hands wrapping around her upper arms and placing her upright again.

"Oh, oh, dear!" Eliza said, her voice breathless and flustered—and a bit on the dramatic side, she knew. She hoped that he couldn't tell how hard she was faking it, or that the fall had been entirely on purpose, a simple ploy to get his attention. "Oh, sir, I'm *so* sorry!" she went on. "I was just going over to the boats there, to take one out on the lake, and I—"

"It's alright, it's alright," John said to her quietly, still holding on to her arms, testing her steadiness on her feet. Seeming assured that she would not somehow go flying once again, he loosened his grip but did not let go. "Are you alright?" he asked her, bending down a bit to see into her still-downcast eyes. "Are you hurt?"

She looked up at him then, into his green eyes, so very like the color of her own, and in that moment, she understood those couples she'd seen strolling around the lake. When her eyes locked with John's, everything around them seemed to disappear—his friends, the group of city folk, the boats, the grass, even the very water itself, even her precious sunshine. Nothing moved, and there were no sounds except the beating of her heart, throbbing in her ears like a drum: *John, John, John,* it told her, repeating the name that she now knew would be with her forever.

"No," she said, her voice sounding tiny and far away to her own ears. As she spoke, their eyes remained locked, as though neither could look away. "No, I'm alright," she went on absently. "Thank you so much for catching me."

"Happy to oblige," he told her, his tone just as distant as hers. He straightened up now but his hands still held her firmly, and from his height—easily a head taller than Eliza— he peered down at her, unblinking, his brow furrowed as if behind it his mind struggled to figure out some great enigma.

"I'm John," he said finally, echoing the cadence that still rang within her, speaking slowly as if compelled to speak his name to her. "John Barrett."

"Eliza Anceaux," she replied, holding her hand up for him to shake, a forward gesture that came to her unconsciously. He simply looked down at it at first, then slowly reached for it, taking it in his own and holding it gently.

"Are you sure you're alright?" he asked her again, as if unable to utter anything else.

Eliza laughed softly at this, but only because she felt it, too: the inexplicable attraction, the magnetic pull that brought them together and rendered any words they could share between themselves meaningless. There *were* no words for this, no way to express what she was feeling, what she had felt from the moment she'd first seen him. And looking up into John's eyes now, standing right in front of him and feeling the warm touch of his hand, she knew for certain that he was feeling it, too.

"Yes," she replied, her voice almost a whisper. "Yes, and thank you again. You are truly a life saver." She paused, not wanting to do what she knew must come next, wishing that they could stay like this forever, hand in hand along the bank of the river basin. Still, reluctantly, she withdrew her hand from his and took a careful step backwards.

"Good day, sir," she said, nodding her head at him, casting her eyes downward in the most ladylike of gestures.

"Ma'am," John replied, bowing his head as well, though his tone belied the confusion all this was causing him.

And then without further ado, Eliza turned and walked away from him. Making her way back up from the water's edge, retracing the path she had taken to get to John, each step was more painful than the last. But still she smiled because she could feel his gaze on her back, searching for her, yearning for her, trying with all its might to call her back to him. And she knew, in her heart of hearts, that things would be different for her now.

John Barrett, she thought, and knew that nothing in her life would be the same.

THREE

That night, John slept fitfully and arose in the morning feeling anxious and distracted, as though he had lost something but could not quite figure out what it was. From the moment he set his feet on the floor his thoughts were racing, trying to retrieve the secret his mind was hiding from him.

"I paid my bill at Jackson's," he muttered as he peered into the cloudy looking glass his mother had hung on the wall in his bedroom, an attempt to add a little decoration to his otherwise Spartan quarters. "I gave James back his copy of *Leaves of Grass*."

As he knotted his narrow, four-in-hand tie around the collar of his white shirt, he silently ran down a list of other items he'd had to remember over the last week or so—favors to return, thank yous to extend, material goods to lend or borrow. John's circle of friends and family was large and active, and he always had something going on with one or another of them. Lately, it seemed, the obligations had been piling up, and he'd been working longer hours as well to make some extra money. It was no wonder, he told himself, that he was feeling so behindhand.

Picking up his vest from the back of a nearby chair and throwing it on, he fastened its buttons slowly, his mind still

15

searching. This all explained his distracted state, but not entirely. There was something else, he thought, another factor that still eluded him. Something he wanted, something he needed, something he'd only recently found and was desperate to keep within his grasp.

He had never felt so frustrated—or so inexplicably excited—in his entire life.

Downstairs, his mother handed him a cup of steaming, black coffee, which he gulped down as quickly as he could— all his early morning ruminations had put him off schedule, and he did not want to be late for work. He never was, and he wasn't going to let a moment of idle pondering ruin that.

"Mother, thank you," he said, stopping to give her a kiss on the cheek as he placed his coffee mug in the sink—a new addition to their kitchen. *Indoor plumbing,* it was called. John wasn't entirely sure he liked it yet.

Running out the door and 'round back to the stable, he exchanged a good-morning wave with his father, who was already out in the fields and probably had been since daybreak. John hadn't gotten his own impeccable work ethic out of thin air; his father had set a lifelong example for him, had taught him that a man worked hard and provided for his family.

"Love and land, son," his father often told him. "Any man who has both will never want for a thing in his life."

Hands on his horse's saddle, about to hoist himself up, John paused. Again there came a tug at his conscience. *Something's missing,* it told him, calling him to stop and think about it some more.

But he had to get to work. So, up and off he went, bringing the horse up to a full gallop in no time. He raced down the dirt road that led into town, letting the cool, early morning air clear his thoughts for him.

Entering the city proper, John pulled on his horse's reins and slowed to a trot, mindful as always of the rest of Savannah's workforce, out bright and early to open their shops, start up the machines at the factories and unload the train cars. These were his people, the ones to whom he related—the industrious, the entrepreneurial, the business-minded. At only nineteen years of age, he already had his plans. He wouldn't be working at the lumberyard his whole life. All he needed was—

"Something," he said to himself, guiding his steed to a stop in the middle of the street as a passel of young women passed before him, carrying books and lunch pails, en route to the nearby schoolhouse. Oblivious to their surroundings, their dresses whirling as they scurried along, laughing and chattering among themselves. John tipped his hat at them and smiled politely.

"Ladies," he said, though none seemed to hear him. Patiently—for a man was always patient when it came to the fairer sex—he waited until they were at a safe distance and then clicked at his horse to move on.

But as it did so, it stopped and began to prance about—not because John told it to but because something, it seemed, had spooked it. Looking around for the cause of his animal's irritation, John pulled the reins up tight, trying to keep it in line. But he saw nothing out of the ordinary, nothing that should have disturbed the horse so.

And then, a plait of brown hair caught his attention. And he remembered a smile, a laugh, a flash of green eyes, the same color as his own.

Oh, sir, I'm so sorry! a quiet voice echoed in his mind. *Thank you so much for catching me.*

"Eliza Anceaux!" he whispered in astonishment, watching as the group of girls ran into the schoolhouse, their backs to him. In the doorway, one paused, turning halfway back toward the street and in profile; he knew it was she. The girl who had fallen on him at the lake. The young woman whose touch had so distracted him.

And in a moment, all of it made sense. The sleeplessness, the anxiety, the disruption of his normal routine. Watching her turn and enter the building, his heart beat faster. He knew who she was now, knew where she was—and knew, with utmost certainty, that he had to see her again. That whatever his future held, Eliza Anceaux would be a part of it.

Suddenly, he knew just what is was he'd been missing.

***

"Eliza," John said softly as he worked on the remains of a hundred-year-old tree, the name falling from his lips in rhythm with his sawing. "Eliza," he repeated as the sawdust fell onto his boots and flew up into his hair, as he pushed and pulled the serrated blade across the wood, its *zip, zip, zip* reverberating against his hands, his arms, his whole body.

John liked his job here at the lumberyard, liked the physicality of it, the way it tired him out by the end of the day. There was honesty in this work—and money, for the man who was willing to put some time into it. Every day, as he sawed and axed and stacked and piled, John thought about how much he had already earned and saved, and how much more he needed to carry out his plans.

A little land and a couple of horses, he always told himself. *That is all I need.*

But on this day, he realized that he'd been wrong. There was something else that he needed. And for the first time since he had started at the lumberyard, he had something besides wages on his mind.

"Eliza," he said again as he drew the saw across the massive tree trunk, but the motion and the thought were interrupted by the loud ringing of a bell—the signal that it was time to break for lunch. While all the other men rushed by him into the workhouse to retrieve their lunch pails, talking and laughing, John stood apart from the camaraderie, his mind on other matters.

"Eliza," he said once more. There had to be something he could do. Some way he could reveal all his thoughts to her.

With a snap of his fingers, he ran into the building and retrieved a pencil and paper, then retreated to the back of the work yard, where a few dirty, old tables and chairs had been set up for meal times. Only a few of his colleagues were out there today—it was a hot one, so most of the men had stayed inside, where it was cooler. Setting himself up at an empty table, John brought the tip of the pencil up to his tongue and then poised it over the paper, waiting for inspiration to hit him. It did not take very long.

"Dear Miss Anceaux," he said aloud as he began to write, then continued on with his letter from there:

> I hope that you will remember our chance meeting at the lake on Tuesday last. You tripped while on your way toward the boats, and I was fortunate enough to be available to break your fall.
>
> Miss Anceaux, I must tell you that since that moment, you have been on my mind. I did not realize it at first, but in a short time I have come to realize what an effect you have had on me. I cannot stop myself from recalling your lovely eyes, and the way they seemed to peer into my very heart, your gentle voice, a sure marker of your inborn kindness, and the soft skin of your hand as I held it in mine. All these remained

etched in my memory, leaving me with a longing to see you once more.

However—and forgive me if I seem forward, but I feel that I must tell you this, if only to gain some understanding of it myself—I felt, as we stood together by the lake, looking into one another's eyes, that there was more to consider than mere outward appearances. There was something unspoken between us, something beyond ourselves, that drew us together. I do believe we have a connection, you and I, Miss Anceaux, though I cannot explain exactly why or what it is. All I can do is hope that you feel the same.

Wishing that this letter finds you well, and that we will indeed meet again. Somehow, I am confident that we will.

Sincerely,
John Barrett

Breathing out a great, slow sigh of relief, John looked at his letter, reading it over one last time. He felt better, less troubled, now that he'd gotten those thoughts out of his system.

"Now," he said to himself, standing up and collecting his writing, "I just have to deliver it."

Squinting up at the sky, at the sun directly above his head, John guessed that he had about twenty minutes of his lunchtime left—just enough to slip out of the yard and back again, before anyone even knew he was gone. And with an image of the schoolhouse around the corner in his mind, he ran inside to put on his tie and jacket. He wanted to look proper, after all, when he ran the most important errand of his life.

FOUR

To Mr. Barrett.

Eliza dipped her pen into the inkwell at the corner of her desk and gathered a large drop of ink, then let it fall onto the name, rubbing the black smudge around until she could no longer see the letters.

Dear Mr. Barrett.

Again, it just didn't sound quite right. Another drop of ink, another swirl of the pen and again it was gone.

Dear John.

Eliza sat back and smiled at the paper on her desk, satisfied that she had found the right opening for the letter she felt so compelled to write.

But what else could she put in it? As she pondered, she turned her head to peer out the nearby window. Outside the schoolhouse the workers' lunch hour had just begun and the street was bustling; people strode by on foot and on horseback, and vendors sold their wares from carts on the corners—fruits and breads, newspapers and tonics, all the things that one might need to pick up in a hurry.

Craning her neck a bit, Eliza strained to get a better look at a group of noisy men gathered just outside the window. Talking and laughing, she could just see the tops of their heads, their ruffled coifs, the dirt smudges on their ears. Their foreheads were tanned, as though they spent most of their days outdoors, and were those bits of sawdust she spied in their hair?

Is one of them my John? she thought, remembering the glimpse she'd stolen of him that morning as he'd paused in the street to let her pass. Unfortunately, too caught up in conversation with her friends, she hadn't realized it was John until she'd passed him by, until she was almost inside the schoolhouse. At that point, her teacher would not let her go back out, but she'd longed to run to him and say hello, to remind him of their meeting the day before, to do or say something that simply would let him know that she had seen him, that she was there. But it was impossible. She'd been ushered into the classroom, and John had been lost to her.

At least, for the time being. All morning the vision of him had danced around her mind—his brown hair, his green eyes, the way he'd pulled his horse to attention before her, so chivalrous, so proper. *Did he see me?* she wondered over and over. *Did he know who I was?* She couldn't help but think that he had, that he wouldn't have stopped like that for just anyone.

"Miss Anceaux," the teacher said from the front of the room, eyeing Eliza suspiciously. "Are you working on your assignment?"

"Oh, yes, ma'am," Eliza said sternly, sitting up straight again and turning back to her desk. Leaning over her paper, lest anyone see it, she dipped her pen in the inkwell and began writing again, quickly and quietly, the words that had been tormenting her restless mind.

Dear John,

I hope that you will remember me, though we have only met twice. Yesterday, at the lake, it was my good fortune to find you waiting to break my fall as I rushed past you, en route to the boat yard. Your exemplary manners and, if I may say so, impressive physical strength kept me upright at a moment when I was most embarrassed by my lack of grace—which, I must confess, was not entirely accidental. I hope that this revelation does not shock you, and that you are instead flattered that a young woman would go to such lengths to make your acquaintance.

Our second meeting, if you could call it that, was just this morning, in the road outside the schoolhouse. I am sorry that I did not realize it was you right away, as I would have liked to stop to talk to you again. I am not sure why, but I feel as though, were we given the chance, we would have much to say to one another. I can (and do!) envision us engaging in long, meaningful conversations about all manner of subjects—life, love, art, business, anything and everything that comes to our minds. I wonder if you see this for us as well.

In closing, John, I will tell you two things. First, I do not hope that there is a third meeting in the stars for us. In fact, I know it to be so. Do not ask me how. It is just a feeling that I have.

Second, please forgive the familiarity of my greeting at the start of this letter, but nothing else I tried seemed quite right. John, I must tell you that from the moment I first saw you I felt as though we were connected. Something draws me to you in the oddest but most delightful way, and I hope—I hope and I pray, truth be told—that you are feeling the same way about me.

Until next time,
Eliza Anceaux

While reading back over the lines she had written, Eliza waved her hand above the paper, fanning the ink to dry it. She grinned to herself, pleased with the thoughts she had expressed and thrilled by the thought of John reading them. She could not say why, not even to herself, but she was just so sure that he would feel the same way about her, that he had sensed the connection between them just as she had. How could he not have? When they'd looked at each other, it had been incredible, powerful...

"*Electric!*" Eliza whispered, looking out the window again, at the people who now hurried back to their workplaces. She shivered at the memory of the *zing* she'd felt when she'd first laid eyes on John, and then again the first time that he'd touched her. She couldn't wait to feel it again. She had to find a way to make it happen.

"The lake," she told herself, squinting up at the sky outside the window. The sun was just coming out, creating a promise of a beautiful afternoon. Surely, on such a day, John would return to the water for a rematch with his boat-racing friends—or, at least, to find Eliza. Wouldn't he?

Eliza paused.

Wouldn't he?

In her doubt, she turned back to the classroom, the dreary, serious reality in front of her. As usual, the teacher was watching and, upon catching her eye, signaled for Eliza to continue with her assignment.

He would, Eliza told herself with a secretive smile, quickly folding up her letter and slipping it into her sleeve. She then opened up her lesson book and pretended to read it, sure that this would be the longest afternoon of her life.

FIVE

As far as Eliza was concerned, there was nothing on earth more beautiful than Savannah in the summertime. By August everything was lush and green as far as the eye could see, with a constant, lingering scent of flowers in the air. At night, the crickets outside her bedroom window lulled her to sleep with their incessant symphony, and in the morning the blazing sun woke her with its heavy, humid warmth.

And every afternoon, whether rain or shine, brought her John, the most glorious of that summer's many gifts.

Since their first meeting almost two months previous, they had seen each other almost every day. Once school let out, Eliza was expected, of course, to help her mother around the house and to keep watch over her younger brothers and sisters. Her days so far had been filled with cooking and cleaning, with laundering clothes and making trips into town to Jackson's mercantile. Often she was busy from dawn until dusk, but she did not mind. She loved her family, and was happy to help where she could.

But no matter how laden with chores she seemed to be, she always, always found time to see John. Even if it could only be a few moments outside the lumber mill when he got out of work, Eliza would be there to smile at him, to hold his hand, to wish him a good evening. Truth be told, it was those small moments that she lived for.

On some days, however, she was more fortunate, and had some time off from her regular routine—a few hours, or even an entire afternoon. When she found herself thus unburdened, of course she made plans with John. So far they had enjoyed long nature walks in the woods near his home, leisurely boat rides on the lake and hour upon hour spent just talking, or just looking into one another's eyes. Often, they met up beneath what they had come to call "our tree"—an enormous, old oak down by the lake, set back from the waterline, its massive, leafy branches creating the perfect secluded setting for them.

This was their plan on one particular Friday afternoon, and so Eliza hurried all morning to complete the tasks her mother had given her. She furiously scrubbed the floors, hung out all the washing to dry and even managed to bake a couple loaves of bread; seeing John, of course, was a great incentive to get things done. By three o'clock, she had not only finished with her work but had packed up a picnic lunch, put on a clean dress and managed to fix her hair in a nice, tidy bun.

"Mother, I'm off to the lake!" she called down the hallway at last, when she was finally ready to leave. Grabbing up her picnic basket with one hand and holding her hat on her head with the other, she added, "I'll be home before dark!"

"Have fun!" her mother called back to her, but Eliza barely heard her. She was already out the front door, heels clicking quickly down the steps and then kicking up a dust cloud as she ran down the road toward the watershed. Far off in the distance, she swore she heard the bell ringing at the lumber mill, signaling the end of the workday, and she ran faster. She wanted to have everything perfect under the oak tree before John got there.

***

"Eliza, darling," she read aloud, holding John's letter out in front of her like an official proclamation. "Though it has only been an hour since we last parted, I feel as though I have not seen you for days. I will sleep tonight dreaming of your lovely face, and of the next moment when I will see you once again. Would it be too soon to say that you have stolen my heart from me?"

Eliza's cheeks flushed as she read these words, as did John's, which did not surprise her—as eloquent as he was on paper, when they spoke of their feelings aloud he always grew a bit abashed. Looking over at him now, she placed a hand gently on his arm, reassuring him that he had nothing of which to be embarrassed.

"John, we've been exchanging such letters every day since the end of June," she told him gently, recalling those first notes they'd given one another. John had written his hastily on his lunch break and left it for Eliza at the schoolhouse, though she had not received it until after class was through. Reading it voraciously, she'd felt emboldened, and had literally raced down to the lake to deliver her own missive.

At the time they had both marveled at the coincidence, at their simultaneous inspirations to write down their feelings for one another. Now, Eliza believed that chance had nothing to do with it.

"Are you not happy with our regular correspondence?" she asked him gently, worried that he tired of their letter writing, a custom that she had come to greatly enjoy.

Lying across the blanket she'd spread out beneath their tree, propping himself up on one elbow, John looked out over the lake, following the movements of some faraway boaters—his friends, perhaps, or another couple out enjoying the perfect, summery weather.

"I am," he said evenly, his eyes still on the water for a moment longer. Then, he turned to Eliza and he smiled, a sudden and beautiful gesture that warmed her more than the bright, orange sun above them ever could. "I was just thinking of some other things that I should have added."

He reached down and caught her hand up in his, then brought it up to his lips, kissing the back of her fingers ever so gently. Eliza brought her other hand, still clutching his letter, up to her heart, which was fluttering like a leaf in the breeze.

"Go on, then," he said to her, replacing her hand on his arm. "Finish your reading."

Bringing the piece of paper back out in front of her, Eliza continued. "When we see one another, I don't just see you, Eliza, but I see my future—and our future together. I see our home, and our family, and all the good and bright things that I want in this world. I would say that I hope you see these things, too, when we are together, but somehow I am sure that you do. I have never known anyone whose thoughts have been so very much like my own."

She paused there, reflecting on that last passage, on the truth of it. As they had grown to know one another, they'd found that their opinions and feelings on so many matters just completely meshed. They both valued family, and love, and honor above all else. They believed in hard work and just rewards, in optimism and charity and kindness. Though they were both young, they had dreamed for quite some time about finding their soul mates, their lifelong partners. More and more, they were realizing that they'd been dreaming about one another.

"Do *you* have a letter for *me* today?" John asked eagerly then, breaking into Eliza's thoughts.

"Oh," she said, feeling a bit startled, "of course I do!" Reaching into the opened picnic basket, she retrieved a folded piece of paper and handed it over to him. As he usually did, he ran it quickly beneath his nose, taking in the delicate perfume with which Eliza always scented her letters.

"Lilacs," he said, and Eliza nodded. It was her favorite—and was quickly becoming his as well.

"Are you going to open it?" Eliza asked him, her eyes wide and eager, as if she couldn't wait for him to reveal the secrets within. He thought about it for a moment, his fingers poised to unfold the note. But then he stopped himself.

"I think I would like to save it," he said, "so that I may read it later, when I'm all alone. So that I can feel as though you are still with me."

Eliza beamed at him. "What a perfectly wonderful idea," she said, imagining him sitting on the front porch of his house, reading her words by candlelight and smiling into the darkness beyond, knowing that although they were apart, they were never truly alone. Day after day, the attraction between them grew stronger, as did their connection, and Eliza was sure that fate had brought them together. Now, she could not remember the time when they had been apart.

Six

"Mother, I don't think I can do my chores today."

Limping into the kitchen, Eliza was aware of her mother's eyes on her back, could see their scrutinizing, penetrating stare.

"And why is that, young lady?" her mother asked, her voice reproachful.

Eliza dropped herself heavily onto a chair and lifted her right leg into the air. "I don't know, Mother, I just woke up with an awful pain in my knee."

Her mother's face changed at that quickly; she put down the bottle of milk she'd been holding and rushed over to see what the problem was. Kneeling down, she pushed Eliza's skirt up past her knee and peeled back her stocking to have a better look at it.

"Hmm, it is a little red," she concluded, running her hand lightly over the joint. "Does it hurt when I press on it?"

"Ow, yes!" Eliza replied, wincing as her mother's fingers poked her tender skin.

"Did you fall down yesterday, or hit your knee on something while you were cleaning?"

Eliza shook her head. "Not that I remember. Maybe I just slept on it wrong…"

As her mother continued to examine the area in question, Eliza looked down at her ministrations, amazed, as always, by her patience. The woman could be a bit authoritarian at times, but Eliza always knew that when she needed her mother, she would be there to give her all the tender loving care that she required.

"Well, you'd better take yourself back up to bed," her mother finally conceded, standing up and smoothing out her apron. "I don't think hobbling around on that bad knee will help it at all. Go on, and I'll bring a cup of tea to you in a bit."

Eliza paused then, slowly rolling her stocking back into place. Her face twisted in thought, she considered how exactly to tell her mother that she couldn't stay in bed until she recovered.

"Mother, I'm supposed to meet John in a little while," she said sheepishly, almost too low for her mother to hear.

"Excuse me?" her mother said, leaning over again.

Eliza looked up at her and smiled, hoping that a little charm would work. "I said I have a date with John, Mother. I'm supposed to bring lunch for him and meet him at the lake."

Her mother straightened up again and just stood there, looking down her nose at Eliza as if pondering just what to do about this awkward situation.

"Well…" she finally said, turning back to her bottle of milk, "I suppose that if you're well enough to do that, you're well enough to help me cook lunch for your father. Get out the flour, now, and let's make some biscuits before he gets in from the field."

Eliza sighed, easing herself back up onto her mysteriously savaged knee. She bounced lightly up and down a couple of times, testing her weight on the injured limb, finding that perhaps it wasn't as bad as she'd thought it was.

At least, that was what she was going to tell herself if that was what it would take for her to see John that day.

***

The summer was coming to an end.

Sitting underneath the great bough of their tree by the lake, Eliza waited for John and thought back on all the afternoons they had spent there together. This scenery would be forever etched in her mind, she was sure, along with the scent of moss and gardenias, and the burn of the sun on her skin. This summer had been the hottest she could remember—though she could barely remember any summer before it, or before John had come into her life.

Peering off into the distance, down the crooked path that led to the lake and into the more public area of the reserve, she began to wonder where exactly her man was, and what was taking him so long. Sure that it was half past noon already, she glanced at the picnic basket where a package of freshly made fried chicken grew rapidly cooler. They had agreed to meet for lunch, had they not? Eliza searched her memories, trying to recall if perhaps they had settled on another day, or a time later in the afternoon, after John was through with work. But nothing came to her. She was positive she was there just as she should be.

"Well, if the man does not come to the mountain," she said at last, standing up gingerly and brushing off her dress, "then the mountain shall be brought down to the man!"

Quickly she rolled up the blanket upon which she'd been sitting and tossed it into the basket, then headed over to where she had left her horse and carriage. Feeling pity on her at last, and knowing how important it was for Eliza to see her beloved, her mother had allowed her to take the cart out instead of walking—an extraordinary favor that Eliza would not soon forget. She would do double the chores the next week to make up for it.

After climbing carefully up into the carriage, Eliza settled herself on its bare, wooden seat, then grabbed up the single horse's reins and gave them a jerk.

"*Hyah!*" she shouted to the old mare, pulling the reins to turn it around onto the roadway into town. If she went that way and John was already headed toward the lake, she'd run into him, and at least get to see him for a minute. If not, she would just continue on to the lumber mill—and, hopefully, find the source of his delay.

***

"Hold on, now, Barrett!" exclaimed one of the young men who surrounded John, holding him upright and inching him across the doctor's office. "Hold on! We're almost there!"

Cursing under his breath, John inhaled deeply and told himself that he had to relax. Fighting against the friends who were trying to help him wouldn't do any good, nor would looking down at his knee, though he desperately wanted to. An enormous amount of pain radiated from it, and he imagined that it must have looked just as bad as it felt.

"Okay, sit down now," the same young man said, helping John to ease onto a cot in the examination room. "Good, now lie down," the man went on, swinging John's injured leg up onto the bed as another friend pushed John's shoulders down.

Closing his eyes for a moment, John let out a deep sigh and tried not to pay attention to the throbbing that spread down his entire right leg. "Is it bad?" he asked no one in particular, his voice low and hoarse, riddled with pain.

"I'll be the judge of that," said old Dr. Sherman, a skinny, balding man in a bright, white shirt and gray-tweed waistcoat. He pushed his way through the crowd of John's coworkers and over to the side of the cot, a small, dull penknife in his hand. He paused, looming over John, blotting out the light pouring in through the window behind him.

"I hope those aren't your good pants, John," the old man said with a dry laugh. "Afraid I'm gonna have to cut 'em open to get a look at ya."

"Do what you have to," John told him, throwing an arm over his eyes, listening to the *rip, rip, rip* of the doctor's knife as it shredded his work pants. A cool breeze hit his inflamed knee and, for a moment, it felt so good that he almost smiled at the sensation, but then the throbbing kicked in again and there was nothing but agony.

"Well, looks like you busted yourself up pretty good there," said Dr. Sherman, poking at the knee with his bony fingers.

"But I think you're in luck, my boy..." He prodded some more, staring up at the ceiling as he did so, his sensitive hands telling him all he needed to know. Finally, he looked back down at John and grinned warmly.

"Doesn't feel like anything is broken. I'll put a good, tight bandage on it, and you'll stay off your feet for a few days, and before you know it you'll be back sawing logs with the best of 'em."

John smiled back at the doctor but there was no joy in it, only annoyance at himself for getting into this mess. It could have been worse, much worse, and he knew that. But he would have to take time off of work, and that meant no pay, and that would throw his plans all off schedule.

But, more importantly, he would miss his lunch date with Eliza.

At the thought of her name, an image of her sweet face jumped into John's mind and for the first time in many hours, he felt nothing but happiness. He could feel the softness of her sandy-blonde hair in his hand, hear the sound of her gentle voice in his ears. Suddenly he smelled moss and gardenias, and he was sitting beneath their tree by the lake, staring into her beautiful eyes as she stared into his. Their gaze was trance-like. He could have looked at her forever.

"Just relax, now," Dr. Sherman told him softly, and so John did. He let the exhaustion of the morning wash over him, let it take away the throbbing pain in his knee. He thought about Eliza, about how much he—yes, about how much he loved her. Had he told her that? In his daze, he couldn't remember. But he would. He had to. He loved her, and he wanted to spend the rest of his life with her, and give her everything that she would ever want or need.

"Eliza," he mumbled, "I love you."

And before he knew it, he had drifted off to sleep.

***

"Where is he?" he heard a voice ask in the outer room, and he reluctantly opened his eyes. Sitting halfway up on the cot, he looked around the examining room. He was alone; all his friends had gone back to work. He couldn't blame them. They all got paid by the hour.

"John!" Eliza called, rushing into the room, her skirts aflurry. She ran to his bedside and knelt down roughly, grabbing his hand and holding it to her face. Her cheek was warm and flushed but also moist, as if she'd been—

"Are you crying?" he asked her, putting a hand to her chin, raising her face so he could see it more clearly. "Eliza, what's wrong? Are you alright? Are you hurt?"

She laughed then, the sound coming out somewhere between a choke and a sob. "John," she repeated, "John, John, John." She looked at him, into his eyes, and paused there as though lost in the sight of him. Still holding his large, rough hand in hers, she brought it up to her lips and kissed it gently. "You're the one who's hurt, silly."

John sat up further then, pulling his hand away from her to steady himself. Looking down, he saw his torn pants, his missing shoe, the thick, white-cotton bandage wrapped around and around the joint of his knee. At least, he realized, the throbbing had stopped.

"Oh, that," he said, relaxing again, and once again grabbing Eliza's hand. He turned on his side a bit to face her, so he could see that beautiful face of hers in the flesh. "That's nothing," he said, smiling at her widely. "Just a scratch, really. Don't you worry your head about it."

Eliza smiled then, too, and John was glad for it; her expression lit up the room brighter than the sun did pouring through the window.

"What on earth happened to you?" she asked, brushing back his hair from his sweaty forehead.

John shrugged, trying to make light of it. He just didn't want to make her worry. "Well, there was a large tree at the lumber mill, a new delivery, and it just didn't want to stay upright. Unfortunately, my knee got in its way."

Eliza paused, and by the look on her face, John could tell she was thinking about something. "When did this happen?" she asked him.

"Oh, a couple hours ago, I guess," he replied. "Why?"

Silently, Eliza glanced down at his bandages, at the same time bringing her hand to rub her own knee—the same one, right side, that John had injured.

"No reason," she replied, her voice distant for a moment, but then she looked back at him.

"No reason," she said again. Then, after a glance over her shoulder to make sure that Dr. Sherman was not around, she leaned in and kissed him.

Suddenly, John was feeling a whole lot better.

SEVEN

Promptly at six-thirty in the evening, John gripped his walking stick and thumped his way up the steps of Eliza's house, his cantankerous right knee groaning at him whenever he lifted it.

"I told you, don't give me trouble tonight," he muttered to it, then laughed at his own ridiculousness. Talking to his own appendage. He blamed it on his nerves.

At the top of the porch the front door lay open, only the screen door keeping the evening's gathering mosquitoes from invading the bright rooms within. From inside the house he could smell meat roasting and hear the quiet chatter of women in the kitchen. Gently resting his stick against the wall, he raised his hand and rapped on the screen's wooden frame with one bare knuckle.

The sounds inside continued unabated, and John reached up to straighten his hat, his tie, his coat. He had dressed slightly more formally than he imagined was called for; it wasn't like he'd never been to dinner at Eliza's before. He was sure, in fact, that if he showed up in his dusty, dirty work trousers and an undershirt he would be welcomed in and given a seat at the head of the table.

But there was something special about this night, something that just seemed to call for his Sunday best.

"John," said Eliza's father warmly as he came toward him through the foyer. Reaching out, he pushed the screen door open, pausing so that John could hobble out of its way. "Good to see you, son. Come in, come right in."

Mr. Anceaux ushered John into the house and straight into the sitting room, where he instructed the young man to sit down immediately on a very cushy, comfortable divan.

"How's the knee doing?" the older man asked as he dragged an ottoman over and lifted John's foot up onto it.

John smiled. From the very first time he'd met Eliza's parents, they had treated him as if he were family already; their warmth and caring were so very comforting, especially when he was a little under the weather, as he was that night—though he was loath to admit it, even to himself.

"Doing better, sir," he replied, adjusting his leg with a barely noticeable wince as Mr. Anceaux took a seat in a nearby chair. "Hardly hurts at all now."

Mr. Anceaux nodded, gazing down at the knee thoughtfully. "I hurt my leg once real bad—an accident with an old plow out in the field. Laid me up for almost a month! I had to hire a man just to come out and do my work for me."

He looked up at John then and the sadness in his eyes was apparent. John knew how important the family farm was to Eliza's father, how dedicated he was to his work. He imagined that he would one day feel the same way about his own land, once he had some, once his plan was in place.

"That must have been hard for you," he commiserated, and Eliza's father nodded in silence.

After a moment, though, he brightened again, as if he'd banished all thoughts of it from his mind. "That injury is, too."

"Yes, I have to admit, I've made a good recovery," John agreed. "Dr. Sherman told me that it could have ended up a lot worse. Of course, he credits Eliza's excellent care for my speedy return to health."

John took his own moment to reflect now, thinking back on the last month since he'd had the accident. Ever since she had found him that day in the doctor's office, Eliza had dedicated so much of her time to nursing him back to health. While he was home from work, she went to his house daily to check on his bandages and change them when need be; she brought him his favorite foods and made sure that he had fresh drinking water in the ewer by his bed. She sat and read to him from some new books she had procured through Mr. Jackson—Arthur Conan Doyle's *The Hound of the Baskervilles* and Owen Wister's *The Virginian*—particularly because she had thought that John might enjoy them. And he had. He could think of nothing more lovely than listening to her speak.

"She is a good girl," Mr. Anceaux said, a sparkle in his eye. Though Eliza was only one of his many children, John had always sensed that her father had a special spot in his heart for her. She was the oldest, the first born, and such an enormous help to her parents. It was obvious that she had been raised well, so it was no wonder that her father took so much pride in her.

"She is," John agreed, then looked down at his lap and began to twist an errant string from his coat round and round his finger. "Mr. Anceaux," he began before he had a chance to lose his nerve, "I was wondering—"

"John, is that you?" Mrs. Anceaux called from the adjacent dining room as she came out and laid down a plate of freshly baked, dark-brown molasses bread. The scent of it, warm and rich, drifted in to John and seemed to swirl around him. He inhaled deeply and felt his mouth begin to water.

"I hope you brought your appetite," she went on from the other room, leaning in through the doorway to smile at him. "Eliza is helping me in the kitchen, but she'll be out to see you shortly."

"Mrs. Anceaux, I haven't eaten all day in anticipation of tonight's feast!" John replied, and it was the truth. Eliza's mother—just as Eliza herself—was a chef of enormous talent. Every meal he'd been offered at their house had left him more than satisfied—and so full he could have rolled himself home. He'd been looking forward to this dinner for most of the week.

"And please," he added, "give Eliza my regards. Tell her I'm enjoying some time with her father and I'll see her at the table when we sit down to partake of the delicious meal you two have prepared for us."

Eliza's mother smiled and nodded at him. "Will do, dear," she said, then turned and headed back into the kitchen, a puff of flour whisking off of her apron as she went.

"Ah, like mother, like daughter," Mr. Anceaux intoned, appreciatively watching his wife going back to her duties. "I could not have asked for a better pair, and I don't know what I would do without either of them."

Turning his attention back to John then, he lowered his brow as if reemerging himself into a serious conversation. "What were you saying, then, John? Before we were interrupted by that bread's distracting aroma?"

John grew serious then as well, clearing his throat and tugging at the tie around his neck; all of a sudden, it seemed to be colluding with his collar to strangle him. He paused, trying to get himself into the right frame of mind.

"Sir," he finally began, deciding to forego the speech he'd practiced earlier at home and just speak from his heart. "I've been thinking... Eliza and I have spent almost every day together since we met, and as you mentioned just now, I, too, cannot imagine my life without her."

He looked squarely at Mr. Anceaux, hoping that the old man would understand his motivation and, surprisingly, not embarrassed in the least to be bearing his soul this way.

Somehow, confessing his love for Eliza had emboldened him.

"She has become my beacon of light in an otherwise dark world," he went on. "And my future, I believe, depends on her. We are so much alike that sometimes it almost frightens me. But I know that we are meant to be together, not just today but forever."

Mr. Anceaux did not answer, but waited for him to continue.

"I love her," John offered, but still no reply.

"Sir, I want to ask for your permission to marry your daughter."

Mr. Anceaux simply looked back at him, his expression neither shocked nor surprised. There was silence for a moment, broken only by the ticking of a grandfather clock in the corner. After a moment, it chimed softly, playing out its song and then sounding three times to mark the quarter of the hour.

John hadn't planned to get into this so early in the evening, but there, he'd done it. There was no taking it back.

As if I would want to, he told himself, then steeled himself for whatever answer was forthcoming.

"Well," Eliza's father began, putting a rough hand up to rub his scruffy chin. For the first time, John noticed that the older man was still in his work clothes; he must have come in from the fields only moments before John had gotten there. Mr. Anceaux always worked from sunup to sundown; he was that dedicated to supporting his family. John hoped that Eliza's father believed he would do the same for Eliza.

For a minute, he began to believe that he would never get an answer, that Eliza's father would leave him hanging in indecision. But then, Mr. Anceaux's face broke out into an enormous smile.

"Of course!" he practically shouted as he rushed toward John to shake his hand, nearly falling over the ottoman in the process. "John Barrett, I couldn't *imagine* a better husband for my eldest daughter—or a finer son-in-law for my wife and myself. We would be so pleased to welcome you into the family. We've just been waiting for you to ask."

Waiting for me to ask? John remarked silently, the wind taken out of him. Had they really already marked him as marriage material, maybe even discussed the possibility of his marrying Eliza? Had Mr. Anceaux or his wife possibly even broached the subject with their daughter?

"Sir, I have to ask you one more thing," John went on hurriedly, with a glance toward the kitchen. The sounds in there were growing louder and he imagined that Eliza and her mother would be bursting into the dining room at any moment, full platters and bowls in hand, one of the younger children following behind to ring the dinner bell.

"Yes, yes, whatever you need!" Mr. Anceaux said, sitting down next John on the divan and putting an arm around his shoulders. John almost laughed at this; the old man's excitement was truly contagious.

"Sir, I have to ask you—to beg you—not to mention this to Eliza. I would like to keep it a secret for now. I would like her to be surprised."

Mr. Anceaux nodded his head vigorously as he actually leaned in for a hug. He seemed unable to contain himself.

"Yes, of course, not a word, not a word!" he said, enfolding John in his arms and clapping him roughly on the back.

And then, John was able to relax. Letting out a deep breath, he raised an arm and patted Mr. Anceaux's shoulder as well.

Well, that was one major hurdle passed.

Now, he just had to find a way to ask Eliza.

Eight

"Six months," Eliza mused, pulling her shawl more tightly around her shoulders and looking up at the sky. The day was a bit overcast but the sun still shone through as best it could; the air was cool but not cold, as was normal for that time of year. "Six *months.*"

She looked down at John, lying on his back on the blanket she'd spread out beneath their tree, his head resting on her leg. He stared up at the cloudy sky, a look of sheer contentment on his face.

"It feels like six *years* to me," he said softly, his gaze turning slowly toward Eliza. Their eyes met and stayed locked on one another, and John smiled. That old familiar feeling, that hypnotic sense he had whenever he looked at Eliza, came back to him now, and he loved it. He wished that he could feel nothing else forever.

"Funny you should say that," Eliza told him, returning his smile, then lifted once again the paper she held in her right hand and resumed her reading. "'It feels like six years to me,'" she recited, "'but even six hundred would not be enough. All the time in the world would not be sufficient for me to tell you how much I love you, Eliza. I cannot live without you; I *refuse* to live without you. We were meant to meet, just as I was meant to be by your side always, supporting you and caring for you and bringing you all the happiness in this life that you deserve. You are beautiful, my dear, and I am so proud to call you mine. With all the love in my heart, John.'"

Staring up at the sky again, John smiled absently, his mind wandering to the sound of his own words read in Eliza's lovely, soothing voice. Despite the pleasant recitation, however, and no matter what he wrote, it always sounded inadequate to him. Words alone never could fully express what he felt in his heart for Eliza. He never had loved someone so completely, never had felt so completed by another human being. He had loved before, or had thought he had, but now he saw that it had all been a folly. What he had with Eliza was true and everlasting.

"And what about *my* letter?" Eliza said to him, breaking him out of his thoughts. Smiling at her once more, he reached into his jacket pocket to retrieve the envelope she'd given him earlier—and then paused. His fingers brushed against the other item in there: small and gold, shiny and beautiful, just like Eliza herself. It was the most important purchase he'd ever made in his life—and the most expensive.

Not yet, he told himself, resisting the urge to tear the gift from his pocket and present it to Eliza immediately. *You've waited for a long time; a few more minutes certainly won't hurt you. Wait until the moment is exactly right.*

So, instead, he withdrew Eliza's letter, opened the envelope and, taking her hand in his, began to read it aloud.

"'My dearest John,'" he began. "'This letter marks the day that we met, six short months ago. I say short because when I look back on them, it seems as though they have flown right by us. Yet, they have been the longest months of my life. We have done so much in such a small space of time—our daily meetings, the books we have read to one another, our picnics, dinners with our families, and, of course, our adventurous boat rides!'"

"Oh, the boat rides!" Eliza exclaimed with a laugh, thinking back on the times when they'd ventured out onto the lake in one of the watershed's rickety old rowboats. She looked out over the water now, at the few brave souls who rowed along its surface, some quick, some drifting at a leisurely pace.

"John, let's take a boat out now," she said impulsively.

He sat up and looked at her. "Now?" he replied, holding her letter up in the air. "I'm not even finished reading yet."

"Oh, that can wait!" Eliza said, growing excited. She snatched her letter from John's hand and folded it up, then pushed it back into his jacket pocket. John gasped, afraid that she might discover the thing he had hidden there, but she withdrew her hand quickly and none the wiser.

"We have all the time in the world for letters," she told him, jumping to her feet and throwing off her shawl. "Come." She reached out a hand to pull John up. "Let's get out there before the sun decides to leave us completely!"

With no say whatsoever in the matter—not that he minded; he had long been in love with Eliza's spontaneity and enthusiasm—John arose and allowed himself to be led downhill toward the makeshift marina, where Eliza pointed out a boat that pleased her. Hauling it out of the row and dragging it across the dirty field toward the water, John smiled.

"Always an adventure with you, my dear," he called to her as she picked up a couple of oars from the nearby boathouse and dragged them over as well.

At the lake's edge, John poised the row boat half in the water, half out, and held out his hand for Eliza to steady herself with as she boarded.

"Thank you, Captain," she told him with a smirk as she placed a foot in the slightly swaying hull, clutching the side of her skirt in her fist to keep from tripping on it.

"M'lady," John replied, tipping an imaginary hat toward her as she settled into the boat at the bow.

Climbing in next, with the oars in his hand, John sat down toward the stern, facing Eliza.

"Are we ready?" he asked her, and she replied with a mischievous smile and a quick nod of her head.

"Then *away we go!*" he shouted as he stuck an oar out into the silt at the edge of the water and pushed off of it with all of his might. Slowly, the boat shifted against the shoreline and entered the waterway in an easy glide.

Eliza laughed softly. She loved that feeling of weightlessness that came on as the boat began to float. "An excellent launch," she told John. "Now, once around the lake, please," she said with an air of overemphasized formality, sitting up straight and proper as she did so. "And please, no splashing. I do not want to ruin my favorite dress."

John grinned back at her, amused, as always, by her teasing. "Aye, aye, miss," he replied, leaning forward and putting all his might into the first full pull of the oars.

For a few minutes, they enjoyed the ride in silence as John steered the row boat out into the middle of the lake and then pulled the oars in, stowing them near his feet. Looking around, he noticed that all the other crafts had gone ashore; no one else was in sight, and they were alone in the middle of the water.

Must be the weather, he thought, glancing up at the sky, which was growing more overcast by the minute.

"John, how far have you ever traveled from home?" Eliza asked him from out of nowhere.

He smiled at her, looking into her eyes for a moment. They were sparkling, as usual, with the glow of curiosity—one of Eliza's strongest and most-compelling character traits. She often came up with random questions like this for him to answer, and he always enjoyed the conversations her questions sparked.

"Well, I went to Virginia once," he replied. "To visit my mother's uncle and his family. They have a house right near the ocean. We went in the summer."

Eliza smiled back at him, returning his gaze. She imagined him on the beach in his swimming clothes as the bright-yellow sun beat down upon him. "Did you like it there?"

"I did," he replied. "Especially at night. The moonlight by the shore is really quite spectacular."

Eliza laughed at that, surprised by his answer. "Oh, is it?" she asked him, looking up into the sky, which was growing oddly darker. She wondered for a moment what time it was, and if it was in fact later than she'd thought. "Better than the good old Savannah moon?"

"Well, of course not," John admitted. "Because the Savannah moon is the one that I share with you."

Eliza's eyes shifted downward, her cheeks blushing as they always did whenever John gave her a compliment.

"Well, then, here's another question for you," she said quietly, folding her hands in her lap and looking back up at him. "If you could take me anywhere in the world...somewhere we could gaze upon the moon together, perhaps...where would we go?"

John thought about this for a moment as he stared out across the lake, at the water and the trees and plants that surrounded it, and in his mind's eye pictured the city that lay just beyond them. He had always loved living in Savannah, had never really wanted to go anywhere else—and felt that doubly so now that Eliza had come into his life. But if he had to… If they had the option… Where could he take his love that would befit her?

He snapped his fingers. "To a tropical island!" he exclaimed, looking back at her, his eyes wide. "A tropical island full of white sands and coconut trees and all the sunshine we could ever want. A place where we could be alone for the rest of our days and enjoy our time together with no interruptions."

"An island," Eliza repeated softly, looking back up at the sky while she considered the idea. More clouds, it appeared, were rolling in from the east, these a little grayer than those already overhead. Rain was on the way, she was sure of it. But for the time being…well, they would be fine.

"You don't think we would get bored of one another?" she asked. "Or get on each other's nerves?"

"Never," John replied immediately. "We would always be happy and carefree—"

"And we would have nothing to argue about except whose turn it was to collect the coconuts," Eliza finished for him, laughing at the thought of their castaway life together.

"Sounds good to me," John said.

"Me, too," Eliza languidly agreed, leaning back a bit against the end of the boat and dangling her left hand into the water, then pulling it back inside quickly.

"So cold!" she said, pressing her fingers into the fold of her skirt to warm them. She looked up at the sky once more, a chill passing through her. It wasn't just the water that had grown cooler but the air as well. She wished that she had brought her shawl out with her.

"Here, let me warm that up for you," John said, enveloping her freezing hand in one of his. He leaned forward a bit to reach her, careful not to change position too rapidly lest he rock the boat and, God forbid, tip them over into the ice-cold lake. But in his movement, he was able to slip his free hand into his coat pocket and deftly extract the secret that he had been hiding there.

And in one swift gesture, he placed it on her finger. A gold band, with a single solitaire diamond. Even without the usual rays of the sun, it positively sparkled—almost as brightly as Eliza's eyes when he looked up at them.

"My love," he said to her, his voice low. Tears welled in the corners of his eyes; emotion choked his throat. He was unsure if he would be able to continue, but knew that he had to. He had to say it. His life depended on it; he could not go on if he did not do this.

The lake was silent. The wind, the birds, the trees— nothing moved. It was as if time had stopped and John and Eliza were the only two left in existence.

"Marry me," he whispered to her, then brought her still-icy hand up to his lips and held it against them.

A moment passed, and then another, and still the silence remained.

"Eliza," John murmured, now pressing the backs of her fingers to his forehead. Had he made a mistake? Had he asked too soon? He could not understand why she was not answering. "Eliza?" he asked again, then tentatively raised his eyes to her.

And she was smiling. And crying. And nodding her head so hard, he thought she might hurt her neck. With her other hand pressed to her mouth to keep back her sobbing, she managed to eke out a tiny, halting, "I will!"

"Oh, Eliza," John exhaled, moving forward onto his knees, the rocking boat be damned. He had to be near her, had to take her in his arms and hold her no matter the consequences.

"You have no idea how happy you have made me," he whispered in her ear as he brushed her hair back from her flushed face. He looked at her for a moment, his hand on her cheek.

This is the face of my wife, he thought, the word causing his heart to skip a beat. *My wife, Eliza.*

"But I do," she whispered back, regaining her voice. "Because I am just as happy—if not more so. Nothing would please me more in this life than being married to you, John."

And then she pulled him close, not even caring who was around to see it. Tightening her arms around him, she buried her face in the shoulder of his jacket, her joyful tears soaking its material.

"Our life is perfect now," she told him. "And it can only get better."

"Eliza, I—" John began but was cut short by a large raindrop landing on his forehead. Reaching up to wipe it away, he cast his eyes upward and was shocked to find an enormous gathering of rainclouds almost right overhead.

"Oh, dear," he said, pulling away from Eliza and moving back toward the stern of the boat. "We'd better head in. Looks like we'll get soaked!"

"I already am!" Eliza said with a laugh, dabbing at her eyes with the sleeve of her jacket. Sitting back against the bow again, she looked up at the sky as well. "You know, I thought it was going to rain," she began but was interrupted by a menacing rumble of thunder.

And then *crack!* Almost immediately, a bolt of lightning crashed not far away, on land but just at the edge of the water.

"John," she began again, and he could hear the fear in her voice. "I think we'd better hurry back to shore."

"Indeed," he agreed, picking up the oars and getting the boat moving once again.

In the ensuing silence, as John navigated them back toward the boat yard, more rain began to fall in huge, violent droplets, soaking their hair and clothing. Eliza did not mind this—it was just a little water, after all—but she was wary of the rest of the storm. It was the thunder and lightning that concerned her.

"We'll be fine, Eliza," John called to her from the other end of the boat, raising his voice to be heard over the splatter of the rain. She smiled at him, comforted by how instinctively he knew what she was feeling.

Still, something nagged at her, creating a knot in the pit of her stomach.

And then the lightning struck again, and all her fears were proven right.

This time the bolt came down in the middle of the water, as if aiming for that particular spot. The voltage gave the lake a sort of a charge, Eliza thought in the few seconds after it happened, causing the water to swell and surge, giving it a life of its own. Wave upon wave rang out from the point of impact, tossing and turning their little boat like a child's toy in the hands of an angry god.

"John, I'm scared," Eliza called to him, but he was busy trying to keep the row boat moving despite the tempestuousness of the water. His rowing, however, didn't seem to be getting them anywhere, and with the rain and the sudden wind and the increasing thunder—

Crrrrrack!

Another bolt of lightning came down, this time right beside the boat, throwing it irretrievably off balance. Eliza screamed and clutched the side, that feeling of weightlessness overwhelming her again. This time, however, it was not pleasant and exciting; it was terrifying, and she had no control over it.

Within seconds, she was thrown into the water, and the waves lapped up over her head.

"John!" she screamed as she came up for air. "John! Don't let me go!" Fearing that the tumultuous water would drag her under, she lifted her arms and frantically tried to swim. She had to get back to him.

We are meant to be together, she told herself, putting every ounce of energy she had into getting back to that boat. *I will not let a thunderstorm tear us apart!*

"Eliza!" John shouted, dropping his oars and immediately diving in after her. "Eliza!" he called again as the storm tried its hardest to push him under. "Eliza!"

Spitting out the rank lake water that filled his mouth even as he tried to keep breathing, John twisted and turned his head this way and that, searching the surface for any sign of his future bride to be, frantically praying that she was alright. Minutes passed, and all he could see was the pummeling rain.

But then the lightning came down again and illuminated the entire grisly scene. In a flash he saw their boat, overturned and drifting off away from him. He saw their oak tree on the far shore, its massive branches swaying in the gale-force winds. He saw the old boat house, its rusty-hinged door flapping and slamming.

And he saw Eliza, mere yards away from him. Floating on the surface of the water, her skirt and her hair spread out all around her like a halo. She was still, calm, as if at peace, though John knew it was much more ghastly than that, for she was face-down, and she made no movement to right herself.

"No!" he cried out. "No!" He could not believe that so suddenly, he had lost the love of his life, his soul mate.

Lifting his face to the dark heavens, he cried, though his tears were lost in the rain.

Why? he questioned silently, unable to form any more words. *Why my Eliza? Is this how it was meant to be?* He could not believe that fate, which had been so kind to bring them together, would now be cruel enough to tear them apart.

But there she was, lifeless. He looked over toward her and pain wrenched his entire body. How would he ever live without Eliza? How would he ever go on?

Crack! came the reply from the sky above as another bolt of lightning touched down on the water mere feet away from John. In the flash, he saw his love for one last time and raised his hand, his drenched jacket weighing it down, to reach for her.

"Eliza," he whispered weakly, and then the waves overtook him.

And at last, they would be together forever.

PART II

NINE

Seattle, Washington, 2009

"Patrick, are you ready? The girls are going to be late!"

In the front hallway, Carolina Anderson looked in the entryway mirror, pulling her straight, blond hair up into a twist and securing it hastily with a clip. Leaning in closer, she peered into the glass and wiped away a tiny smudge of mascara that had strayed down onto her cheek.

"Losing your touch, old lady," she mumbled to herself, checking the rest of her face for any other slip-ups. She wore minimal make-up, just enough to highlight her sharp-green eyes, her delicate cheekbones. A bit of blush here and a swish of lip gloss there and she was done. But sometimes, when she was in a rush, accidents happened...

"Patrick!" she called again, stepping back now and smoothing down her tailored, black suit jacket with her palms. Reaching up, she adjusted the collar of her white shirt and her clutch of long necklaces, silver and black and gold.

Well, you don't look too *bad for forty-two,* she told herself, taking a moment to appreciate how well this new suit fit her. All those long, early morning power walks were paying off. She was toned, svelte and naturally petite—and feeling pretty good about her looks, age be damned.

She smiled and turned away from the mirror, her morning ritual complete.

"Pat—"

"Coming, Mother," said her seventeen-year-old son as he bounded down the stairs, backpack swinging from his shoulder. "And don't worry, no one will be late."

She sauntered toward him, her high heels clicking on the hardwood floor and resounding off the high foyer ceiling. Pulling a ring of keys from her jacket pocket, she dangled them on an outstretched finger, keeping them just out of the boy's reach.

"Are you sure you're ready for this?"

He smiled at her, the same big, beaming grin he'd had since he was a boy. Reaching up, Carolina smoothed back his hair, wavy like his father's.

Patrick leaned over and gave her a quick peck on the cheek. "Readier than you will ever know."

She smiled back at her son, glad to see him so happy. Patrick had always been such a serious boy, so studious and responsible, so wise. Perhaps that was why Carolina had felt it was alright to let him begin driving his younger sisters— Lindsay, sixteen, and Alexis, twelve—to school a couple times a week, on days when he had to stay late in the afternoons for hockey practice. Then, he could just drive himself home, rather than waiting for Carolina to get there.

He reached for the keys. Instinctively, she snatched them back into her fist.

"No speeding," she warned him. "I don't care if you're all late. You drive the limit and not one mile over, understood?"

"Yes, Mom," Patrick replied gently, not even trying to sound like he wasn't patronizing her.

Reaching up, she tousled his hair, then released the key ring to him. "I know you'll be fine," she said, following him into the kitchen as he turned to go. "But you can't blame me for worrying, now, can you?"

"Worrying about what?" In the kitchen, Carolina's husband, David, was standing at the island in the middle of the room, newspaper in one hand and mug of coffee in the other. He didn't look up at her as he spoke, but continued scanning the headlines.

As Patrick ran out the door, Carolina followed him, pausing just inside the house. She raised a hand and waved at her daughters, who were already in the car, belted in and waiting to leave.

"Bye, girls, love you!" she called to them. "You too, Pat!" she added as he backed the car out, and then they were gone.

"Worrying about what?" David repeated, now standing behind her. He still sipped on his coffee but had replaced the newspaper with his briefcase.

Turning to look at him, Carolina's lips stretched into an involuntary smile. After twenty-one years of marriage, she still found that face of his so comforting, his smile so handsome. He still cut quite a dashing figure in his suit and tie; in fact, every year he looked more distinguished. More like the CEO that he was.

"You know," she told him, putting an arm around his neck and pulling him in for a hug. "Everything and nothing all at once."

"Hey, watch the make-up." David backed up from her abruptly, bringing a hand up to brush his shoulder. She watched his preening, a sinking feeling growing in the pit of her stomach. What he'd said to her hadn't been mean, just off-hand and maybe slightly inconsiderate. If he'd been thinking more about her and less about a speck of powder on his suit, he might have seen that she was feeling a little needy, and that a hug could have put her mind at ease.

"Hey, don't worry about Patrick." David kissed her goodbye, then handed her his coffee cup and disappeared through the doorway and out of the house. Carolina watched him get into his BMW and speed off, cell phone already in his hand. He probably had a conference call scheduled for the drive in. Just Carolina's SUV was left in the carport.

Moving back into the kitchen, she pulled her own cell phone out of her jacket pocket and checked the time: ten minutes until she had to get out of there herself. One of the nice things about owning her own business—an advertising agency, one of the busiest in the city—was that she could set her own hours.

She laughed at herself. "So why aren't I going in at noon and leaving at three?" she wondered aloud, then busied herself with picking up the dishes the children had left scattered across the table.

Trundling across the room with a load of half-full cereal bowls and sticky-rimmed juice glasses, she stacked them in the sink, then paused to look out the window onto their massive property. The pool. The three-car garage. The landscaping—Japanese maple trees, hydrangea bushes in bloom, a koi pond with a bridge. A deck, a barbecue the size of a battleship.

Carolina sighed, wondering why sometimes she just didn't feel like it was enough.

She shook her head to rid it of these thoughts, then moved across the room again and into the small office off the side of the eating area. She and David each had their own separate offices down the hallway, for those nights—and there were many—when they brought their work home with them. This was just a little work station, a place for the phone, the corkboard with their bills tacked to it, the in and out boxes for mail and other messages.

Sitting down in the rolling chair behind the room's small desk, Carolina picked up a stack of unopened envelopes and flipped through them. A letter from the local business-owners' association; something from a national advertising society in which she was a nominal member. Something from David's alumni association; a notice from Alexis' tennis club. A postcard from her friend Janet, who was in Tahiti, and another from Ann on vacation in Brazil. Three mailers from various charities she had supported in the past.

So much correspondence, so many words. "I sure lead a full life on paper."

Putting aside the rest of the mail, she kept the charity envelopes and went through them one by one. She spent a lot of her free time—and her business time as well, when the opportunities arose—supporting various causes, from local animal shelters to helping the homeless to preserving the parks and gardens of greater Seattle. Being so well off herself, she believed in giving something back to her community, to society, to the world. Charity work made her feel a little more whole, as if she were doing something that mattered.

At the very least, it filled up her time so that she just didn't have to stop and think too much.

"Seattle Cancer Coalition," she said at the last envelope, a familiar logo stamped on its reverse. This was one of her favorites, a group that raised money for research into all forms of the disease. Her beloved grandmother had succumbed to colon cancer several years earlier, so this charity held a special place in Carolina's heart. She always did whatever she could to help them.

Tearing open the envelope, she took out the letter and scanned it quickly, standing up and moving back into the kitchen as she did so.

"Annual fundraising dinner," she read as she retrieved her bag and keys by the door. "May twenty-fifth, eight o'clock."

She paused, free hand on the doorknob.

"May twenty-fifth."

Pulling out her cell phone one more time, she clicked on the touchscreen and looked at the date.

"Damn it! That's tonight!"

She hoped she still had time to RSVP.

TEN

"There you go, Mrs. Hamilton. That should have you feeling better in no time." Taking care to put the Band-aid loosely over the spot where he'd administered the shot of antibiotics, Dr. Michael Sanford smiled gently. "Knock that nasty old flu right out of your system."

Sitting on the exam table, the elderly woman grinned back at him, her false teeth large and white. "Oh, thank you so much, Dr. Sanford." She put a quivering hand on his arm, a grandmotherly gesture that he couldn't help but enjoy. "You saved my life yet again."

At that, he laughed, but kindly and genuinely, not in the patronizing way that many medical professionals seemed to have. Michael Sanford was indeed, and sadly, a rarity: a family doctor more concerned with his patients' well-being than with billing codes or insurance—or his golf game.

"Whatever I can do to help," he told her, offering his strong hand to help her down from the table. She grabbed it, then gingerly slid her feet down to the stepstool and then the floor. Standing before him, the top of her head barely reached the level of his chest.

She looked up at him, her eyes twinkling. "You know, with your dark hair and eyes, you look an awful lot like my late husband." She reached up and gripped his muscled arm.

65

"Though you're in much better shape than Howard ever was!"

At that, Michael really laughed. "Okay, Mrs. Hamilton, I think you're feeling better already." He put a hand on her shoulder and gently urged her toward the door. "You see Marissa out front and she'll set up a follow-up appointment for you, okay?"

"Okay," the woman replied, giggling to herself as she went out into the waiting room.

Shaking his head and still smiling at the older woman's rambunctiousness, Michael walked out of the exam room and down the hall to his office. He checked his watch; noon already, time for lunch. He went into his office and closed the door.

Once alone, he let out a long, tired sigh as he pulled off his white coat and hung it on a hook on the back of the door. He walked slowly over to his desk and sat down roughly in his creaky, old wooden chair. It moaned in disagreement as he leaned back in it and swirled around to face the open window. It was a beautiful spring day outside. He couldn't wait to get out there on his bike once he was through with patients for the day.

"Whenever that might be," he said, glancing at his watch again. Michael rarely stopped to eat while he was at work—too much to do, too many people to help. Instead, he spent his lunch hours catching up on paperwork, transcribing patient notes and signing off on prescriptions and other requests. This day, he had a whole stack of papers before him.

"First things first, though." He picked up the phone and quickly dialed a number, then waited as it rang on the other end. "Hey, honey," he said when his wife answered. "How's everything going? Just had a minute so I thought I would call you."

"Everything's good," she said, though there was no particular enthusiasm in her voice. In the background, Michael heard a commotion; it was lunchtime at the elementary school where Julie taught, and she must have had her class out on the playground.

"Any news about Josh's band practice tonight?" he asked, swinging around to gaze out the window again. The sunshine was almost blinding. He reached over and unlocked the window with a satisfying click.

"No, you know Josh. He won't tell me until the last minute and he needs a ride, no matter how much I nag him."

Michael laughed a little and nodded—that was their son. At eighteen years old, he loved nothing more than his guitar and making his parents' lives infinitely more complicated. He was a good kid but fiercely independent. He did what he wanted when he wanted to, and Michael sort of admired that, though he had to admit it was frustrating at times.

"And Emily? Any plans for tonight?" With his free hand he nudged the windowpane upward and, all at once, a rush of sweet, fresh air poured in on him. He closed his eyes and breathed in deeply. This was his favorite time of year, when everything was about to become new again.

"Not that I know of," Julie replied, then shouted something to one of the kids in the background. She sounded irritated, as she often did, especially lately, and not just with her students but with Michael as well. This bothered him a little bit; he was always so even-keeled, and he tried to be upbeat in all situations. All his life he'd been an optimist at heart, and it shone through in everything he did. Always had and, he hoped, always would.

In the twenty years that he'd been married to Julie, he'd always been able to spread a little sunshine her way when she seemed a little manic. She was a true type-A personality, super organized and always on the go. In many ways, that was good; Michael had never paid a bill late since he'd met her. But often, especially in the last few years, it had started to get to him. As they both grew older—not that forty-three was old, but he wasn't a kid anymore—he just wanted a peaceful life, and to enjoy the home and family that they had built together. Julie, on the other hand, just wanted to keep on running.

"Well, maybe we can all do something together," he offered with a faint smile. Emily, their daughter, was sixteen but still very attached to her father. She was always up for spending time with him and with her mother as well—the problem was getting Julie to commit. She always had something to do, some errands to run, just something to take care of. Michael really had no hope that she would make time for either of them that evening.

"Okay, we'll see. I gotta go. Love you, bye." Julie breathed out her response in a rush, then hung up her cell phone. Michael held the dead receiver to his ear for a moment, then turned and dropped it back into its cradle.

"Love you, too," he said quietly, then turned his attention to the paperwork that awaited him.

He got through one patient chart before there was an impatient knock on his office door.

Putting down his pen, he leaned back in his chair, which creaked its concern. Folding his hands across his midsection, he cleared his throat. "Come in," he called out, and the door swung immediately open.

"Mike, you pick up your suit yet?"

"Scott," he said, greeting his partner in the medical practice. "Dr. Butler." He stalled for time, because he had no idea what the guy was talking about. "Sorry," he said at last. "My suit for what?"

Coming fully into the office, Scott grinned at him, that big, goofy smile that let Michael know he had messed something up. The two doctors had worked together for a decade; they knew each other pretty well. They both had pretty healthy senses of humor, too, and took some pleasure in ribbing each other when they messed up on something.

"Your suit! Did you get it from the dry cleaner's?" Scott repeated, taking a seat in front of the desk. The chairs there were a little newer, and leather; his creaked when he sat but in a more pleasing and less menacing way than Michael's did. "For the—the *thing* tonight!"

Michael laughed and shook his head. He twisted left to right in his chair and put his hands up, interlacing his fingers behind his head. He glanced back out the window again, a fleeting image of his bike going through his mind. "I give," he said, turning back to his partner. "What thing? I have no idea what you're talking about."

Shaking his head in mock disbelief, Scott looked at him with the most shaming gaze he could muster. "How could you, Dr. Sanford? It's only the most important social event of the year. Or, at least, of the week."

"Or of the night? How long are you going to keep me in the dark here?"

"Alright, alright." Scott stood up and straightened out his white coat, then pulled his folded-up stethoscope from its pocket. Gripping it in one hand, he shook its earpieces in Michael's direction. "The fundraising dinner for the Seattle Cancer Coalition. Your chance to eat overpriced buffet food and schmooze with the city's richest and most influential, all while giving up your hard-earned money for a good cause."

"Oh, *that*." Michael remembered now. He hadn't wanted to go to this dinner at all when he'd gotten the invitation; he just wasn't a fundraiser kind of guy. He definitely donated to the charity both monetarily and with whatever time he could manage to give. But Scott had talked him into it. For all his sarcasm, he was actually really into giving back to his community, and he had a lot of contacts in the local philanthropic community. All of them would be there.

Maybe you can make some friends, Scott had told him back then, trying to convince him to go along. *I can introduce you to plenty of really nice people.*

"I don't know," Michael said now, putting his arms down and leaning forward onto his desk once again. He picked up his pen and looked absently at the paperwork before him. "I don't know if I'll make it."

"Aw, come on!" Scott exclaimed, throwing his hands in the air and beginning to pace. "You can't back out on me now! You're my date! I can't make it alone, Mike."

Looking up at him, Michael raised his eyebrows and stifled the laugh he felt rising in his throat. "I think you can," he replied. "You are one of if not *the* most social person that I know."

"And you're the biggest stick in the mud *I* know." Scott peered at him, narrowing his eyes conspiratorially. "What if I pick up your suit for you? Would that help you out any?"

Michael sighed and tossed his pen onto the desk again. He ran a hand through his dark-brown hair. It was a little long on the top; he thought about when he might have time to go get it cut. Finally, he looked up at Scott, his face set in resignation. "Yes," he said, "yes, it would help me. If you could pick up my suit, I would appreciate it." He looked at his watch again. "What time does this *thing* start tonight?"

Scott clapped his hands once loudly, a smile spreading from ear to ear across his face. "Eight o'clock. Don't you worry about a thing. I'll get your suit, I'll bring it here, we can go right from work. I'll even be the designated driver, how about that?"

Michael smiled at him warmly. Little bit crazy though Scott was, he was a good friend. He was pushy, especially when it came to getting Michael to do things that were good for himself. But Michael appreciated it; it was nice to know that someone was looking out for him.

"Sounds good," he replied. "Now, get out of here so I can finish this paperwork, or none of us will ever get anywhere."

ELEVEN

"Did you pack your running shoes?"

In the master bedroom, David had a week's worth of clothes laid out across the bed—suits, shirts, socks and underwear with the occasional T-shirts and jeans thrown in for good measure. From the other side of the room, just inside the doorway of the walk-in closet, Carolina looked over his collection.

"And a hat? You know it can get chilly in the morning out in Colorado."

"Yes and yes," David replied, folding a tie and placing it carefully inside his suitcase. He looked over at her and smiled. "I'm all set. Thanks for picking up my dry cleaning this afternoon."

She smiled back, calmly and perfunctorily, as she reached under her hair, which she wore long and loose, to put on an earring. "No problem." After fastening the second earring, she retreated into the closet to find a pair of shoes.

Gone for another week, she thought as she absently perused her shelf of high heels, her mind racing about what she would do while her husband was away. He often went on business trips that kept them separated for fairly long stretches of time; this one was actually a bit on the short side. She would miss him, in a way, though not like she used to pine for him when they were first married and he was just getting started in the business world. Back then, every moment they'd been apart had been like a lifetime for her. They'd been young then; maybe too young, she often mused.

These days, she had to admit, when he went away, she simply looked forward to all the time she'd have to herself.

"First I'll go out for a nice dinner with my long-lost girlfriends," she said to herself, picking up a pair of patent-leather heels to match her little black dress. "And then take a long, hot bubble bath."

After putting the shoes on her feet, she went back out into the bedroom and smiled once again at her husband, who had almost finished his packing. And for a moment, she felt a little bit bad about the plans she'd been making. What with taking care of him and their kids, and running the household and her business on top of that, she rarely had a moment to herself, much less an evening to catch up with her friends. She made every effort to see them when she could, but it wasn't as often as she liked. But what could she do about it?

Nothing, she reminded herself silently. There was nothing she could do, or at least nothing she was willing to do. This was the life she had made for herself, and she was nothing if not responsible. She understood that married couples sometimes grew apart as they aged, but she always tried to remain positive and told herself that this was not the road that she and David were meant to go down.

She just hated to think that a sense of responsibility— not love, passion or commitment—was all that kept her and David together anymore. But, more and more, as the years wore on, she began to think that this was something like the truth. They loved each other, but how long had it been since she'd felt like they were *in love?* The man she'd fallen in love with then was certainly not the man she knew now.

"Honey, do you know where my travel toothbrush is?" David asked her as he headed into the bathroom, shaving kit in hand. He paused in the doorway, awaiting her answer, and she looked at him. Backlit by the track lighting above the sink, his face half hidden in shadow, he looked older, more tired than she thought he should be. He was still handsome, still had that boyish charm in his eyes that she'd been so attracted to some twenty-odd years before. But he was just David now. Not the love of her life. Just the man with whom she shared a bed when they both happened to be in town at the same time.

"Second drawer under the sink," she replied, turning her eyes away as she picked up her clutch from her bureau. "I'm off to the fundraiser. There's dinner for you and the kids in the oven."

**

It was funny how at home Carolina felt in a room full of strangers in tuxedos and cocktail dresses.

"How *are* you?" one woman cooed at her, touching her arm lightly as Carolina walked by her. The woman was older, silver hair cut in a sleek bob, a string of diamonds glittering at her neck. "So good to *see* you!"

"You too!" Carolina replied, smiling so brightly it made her squint. She had no idea who this lady was, but that didn't matter. They were all there to support a good cause, right? A little temporary amnesia when it came to names and faces could be forgiven.

"Carolina," another woman called from a nearby table. "Over here!"

Smiling for real now, Carolina waved at Katherine, her assistant from work. Young and slim, tall and willowy, she looked fantastic in a bright-red halter number, revealing her bony, pale shoulders. Her dark hair was swept into a simple updo.

"Hi," Carolina said, greeting her with a quick hug. "How's everything going? Who have you seen?"

"Oh, all the usual people," Katherine said with a laugh. She and Carolina often went to these events together, and they knew all the regulars. To Carolina, it was like one big family—some there to truly support the cause, some just there because of an interest in philanthropy in general.

And then some, she thought, spying a new face, a man she had never seen at a fundraiser before, *who just don't want to be here at all.*

"Do you know who that is?" she asked Katherine, nodding her head coyly in the direction of this solitary partygoer, standing at the bar all alone, nursing a drink. He was handsome—tall, dark-brown hair, dark eyes, very rugged looking but refined in a tailored, three-piece suit, black with a red-satin tie.

Katherine looked at him as well for a moment. "No idea," she purred. "But I'd certainly like to. Let me ask around. I'll get the scoop on him." And with that, she flitted away, off into the crowd.

Standing at the table by herself, Carolina leaned against an empty chair and considered her options. *I could go talk to him...or I could not.* She stared at the handsome stranger, at the way he lifted his glass, the way his fingers wrapped around it. The way he drank, then crushed a piece of ice between his teeth. Everything about him seemed sort of—

"Mesmerizing," she said in a low voice as the rest of the room seemed to drop away from around her. Suddenly, there were no chattering socialites, no heated discussions, no tinny, monotonous laughter. The smell of the food the servers had just started carrying out from the kitchen no longer wafted around her head; the clink of glasses as people toasted one another failed to ring in her ears. All of a sudden, there was nothing else but her and him, as if they were connected somehow.

And as if there were a line connecting them both across the room, Carolina began to move straight toward him, her gaze unfailing. She couldn't have stopped herself even if she'd wanted to.

"Oh!" she exclaimed, startled when she finally bumped into him, as if she didn't know how she had made it all the way there. She grabbed his arm, his bicep, and squeezed—though that was very conscious. Seeing his muscles straining against the fabric of his jacket, she'd had to touch them, to feel the strength this unknown man possessed. She let her hand linger for a moment but then pulled it away quickly.

Shame on you, she told herself, wiping her sweaty palm against her dress. Feeling awkward now, she looked down at her feet and tried to figure out how to get out of this one.

"Are you okay?" he asked then, grabbing her with his free hand. Warm and sure, his fingers wrapped around her upper arm as if to steady her. His voice was deep and smooth.

Looking up slowly, Carolina met his gaze for the first time, and, inexplicably, something fluttered in her stomach. Looking deeply into his eyes, she felt so drawn to him, and she couldn't look away.

After a few moments, she realized that he couldn't either.

"Are you okay?" he repeated in almost a whisper, his brows lowering.

She nodded absently, almost unaware that she was even doing it. "Yes," she replied. "I'm okay."

Slowly, out of habit, she raised up her hand to offer it for a shake. "Carolina Anderson," she said, still gazing into his eyes. She felt as if she were in a trance.

He curled one corner of his mouth up into a half grin as he put his glass down on the bar and took her hand. His fingers were cold and damp, but his skin was so soft, such the opposite of what Carolina had expected.

"Michael Sanford," he replied, then quickly added, "have we met somewhere before?"

Reaching back into her memories, Carolina tried to remember where she'd seen his face before. He looked as familiar to her as she did, apparently, to him. Had it been at another fundraiser? Some professional function? Had she seen him at the grocery store, or while dropping one of the kids off at school? Nothing rang a bell. Still, she felt like she'd known him before this chance encounter.

Coming up with nothing, though, she shook her head. "Not that I recall." Realizing that she still held on to his hand, she withdrew hers with a small laugh. "So, um, what are you doing here?"

At that, he laughed as well. "Supporting the Seattle Cancer Coalition…?" He raised his eyebrows and picked up his drink again, the smile on his face belying his amusement with her question.

"Right." Carolina raised her hand and knocked on her own head, then rolled her eyes—the universal *what was I thinking?* sign. "What I *meant* was, I haven't seen you at any functions before. Are you new to the city charity circuit?"

Michael looked off over her head—an easy feat for him, she supposed, since he stood almost a head taller than her—as if searching the room for someone or something. "No," he replied, not finding what he was looking for, returning his gaze to her instead. "I've been a supporter for a while. I just usually don't go to the dinners. My partner dragged me here."   Carolina's heart sank. "Your partner?"

"Yeah, in my medical practice. I'm a doctor." Reaching to the inside pocket of his jacket, Michael withdrew a business card and held it out to her between his fore and middle fingers.

Carolina took it and read it over: *Michael Sanford, MD, family practitioner.* She let out a sigh of relief.

"A doctor," she said, opening her purse and taking out one of her own business cards, then handing it to him. "I own an advertising agency."

As he perused the card, he raised his eyebrows and nodded his head. "Very impressive, Miss Anderson!" he said playfully, looking back to her and smiling. Carolina felt her cheeks blush but she shook it off.

Brushing her hair back with her hand and standing up straighter, she reminded herself, *You're just networking here, nothing more and nothing less.*

But then she looked at his eyes again, and something in the pit of her stomach tugged her toward him. She took a step forward, bridging the gap between their bodies.

"So, we don't know each other," she said, still looking at him.

He shook his head. "No, afraid we don't."

There was a moment's pause, and then Carolina shook herself out of the trance again. She cleared her throat. "Do you do a lot of work with the cancer coalition?"

Pulling his own gaze away from her, Michael motioned to the bartender for another drink, and for a second to share with Carolina. "A fair amount. I distribute some of their literature to my patients. Especially the older folks who could really benefit from the programs that they offer."

"That's great," Carolina replied, taking the drink that the bartender offered her and knocking back a swig of it, trying not to wince as the scotch tore its way down her throat. "I try to work them into what I do whenever I can as well. Partnerships and whatnot."

"Really." Michael leaned an elbow against the bar, his stance becoming decidedly more casual. "I'd love to hear more about that."

Carolina smiled at him, lowering her gaze again in embarrassment. His interest in her—though it was only in her work—made her downright nervous. An image of David flashed through her mind, and her cheeks flushed all the more.

But this is harmless, she told herself. *We're just talking about work.*

"Why don't we meet up for coffee sometime and discuss it? Maybe we can even collaborate on some promotion ourselves."

She'd said it before she'd even thought it, the words flying recklessly off her lips. And before she knew what was happening, Michael was agreeing to it. They didn't set a date—that would have been too forward, she thought, too much like...well, a date—but she was promising to call him the following week, and to see what their availability was then.

Just the normal networking that goes on at these parties, she told herself as she shook his hand once more. *Just doing something to help the coalition.*

Their hands lingered, their eyes almost unwilling to part.

But still, I know him from somewhere, Carolina thought, then excused herself before she made any more promises she couldn't keep.

TWELVE

"What's this?"

Pausing in the mud room, Michael kicked off his biking shoes and tossed his helmet on a nearby bench. He ran a hand through his hair and wiped the sweat off his forehead with the sleeve of his shirt as he readied himself for the assault.

"What's what?" he finally called back, trying to keep his voice light.

In the kitchen, his wife, Julie, did not respond. He heard a cupboard open and close, heard the water go on and off. He sighed as he undid the Velcro on the backs of his fingerless gloves, peeling them off his hands and throwing them into his upturned helmet.

"Jules?" he called again, fearing the worst. When she started a conversation but didn't answer him, when she lingered just out of his sight, he knew that there was something really bothering her. She was pissed off about something, and she was trying to make him come to her to find out just what it was.

"My wife," he muttered to himself bemusedly. "She's just a little bit controlling."

Stepping into the kitchen, he put a big smile on his face and went directly over to her for a kiss. Seeing him leaning in and knowing what he wanted, she only offered her cheek, a brush-off if ever there was one.

"What's going on?" he asked her, again making his voice more upbeat than he really felt. He'd just had a nice, long bike ride first thing in the morning, one of his favorite activities on earth. It was another beautiful spring day outside, plenty of sun and blue sky, birds chirping and flowers blooming and everything. He couldn't have asked for a more perfect start to his day. Now, though, it seemed like a storm cloud was moving in over him.

From the front pocket of her jeans, Julie produced a business card, and she flicked it up in front of his face. "This," she said, waving it back and forth. "I found it in the pocket of your suit jacket when I was getting it ready for the dry cleaner's." She turned the card around and raised her eyebrows at it. "Carolina Anderson." She looked back at him. "Who is that?"

A sudden flush of blood came to Michael's cheeks and he put a hand up, rubbing his face as if thinking. "Carolina," he said, the rush now swirling around his brain. He hadn't said her name aloud before, but he'd been thinking about it silently all week, ever since that fundraiser. "Carolina." He chanced saying it again, enjoying the way the name felt rolling off of his lips.

He shrugged then, looking at Julie with a smile. "Just someone I met at that cancer coalition dinner last week," he said, moving over toward the refrigerator to grab a bottle of water. "She runs some ad agency downtown. Does a lot of work with the coalition. Thought we might be able to do some project together for it."

Julie was silent, her eyes moving back and forth between him and the business card. "What kind of project?"

In the middle of a large gulp of water, Michael shrugged again. "Don't know, really," he said, wiping a few droplets of water from his mouth with the back of his hand. "I told her that I hand out coalition literature to my patients sometimes and she thought maybe we could come up with something better in that area, pamphlets or brochures or something."

Still silent, Julie at last put the business card down on the table. "I know it's for a good cause and all, but you already spend so much time out on your damn bike, I hardly ever see you." She crossed her arms over her chest and screwed her face up like a petulant child. "How much more of your time is this going to take away from your family?"

Plastering that smile on his face again, Michael reminded himself not to let her get to him. A type-A personality all the way, Julie had always been prone to hyperbole and drama. Yes, he liked to ride his bike when the weather was good, but he limited it mostly to early mornings, when there wasn't much going on at home anyway. If she needed him there, he was there; he would always put his bike aside for his wife or their children. Maybe he'd stayed out a little long that morning, but it had just been so nice outside, he'd lost track of time.

"I won't dedicate my life to it," he said, then walked over to her slowly. Putting his arms around her, he kissed her forehead. "Don't worry, okay? You know you and the kids are always first for me. I wouldn't put anything between us."

In his embrace, Julie softened; she put her arms around him and rested her face against his chest. "You need a shower," she told him, but her voice was kinder now, not as shrill as it had been when she suspected him of—

Of what? he wondered to himself. Cheating on her? He would never do that...or, at least, never thought he would. He had a perfect life here, momentarily stressed-out wife notwithstanding.

Still, there was just something about Carolina he couldn't get out of his mind.

***

Straightening his tie as he ran into the kitchen, Michael glanced at the clock on the wall—eight forty-five, just half an hour before his first patient would arrive at the office.

"No problem," he told himself, fixing his collar. "Twenty-minute drive and an assigned parking spot. Plenty of time to—"

As he reached for his wallet and keys on the nearby counter, he paused, his eyes falling upon the business card Julie had left on the table.

Carolina, he thought, the name ringing in his ears again, the heat flowing up into his face. *Carolina.* He moved closer to the table, unable to take his eyes of that damned business card.

"Why don't we meet up for coffee sometime?" she'd asked him, her green eyes sparkling in the low light of the banquet room. When she'd smiled at him, he'd had to prop himself up against the bar. What was it about her that had made him literally weak in the knees?

Reaching out his hand for the card now, he paused, and he shook his head—just as he had done a hundred times in the last week. He wanted to call her, wanted to see her, but he'd been putting it off because he just didn't know where it would lead him. Grabbing a coffee together wasn't a big commitment or even a sign of anything; maybe this whole charity idea was for real. Maybe he was reading too much into the way that she looked at him, the way that he'd looked back at her.

He shook his head again. *I know I'm not,* he told himself. There had been no mistake about the attraction between them. Whatever it was, whatever the reason, he had to find out.

Closing his eyes, he moved his fingers closer to the table and felt for the business card. Catching its sharp corner, he snapped it up and, before he knew what was happening, before he could tell himself that he was being crazy, he had his cell phone out of his pocket.

Still free for that coffee? he wrote quickly in a text message, then entered her phone number and hit the "send" button. Turning back to the counter, he grabbed up his wallet and keys and headed out of the house.

"Keep moving," he told himself, feeling a knot forming in the pit of his stomach. If he kept moving, he wouldn't have to think about what he was doing.

As he opened his car door, however, he stopped: His cell phone was chiming in his pocket. Slowly, he put his hand in and withdrew it; even more slowly, he flipped the phone open and clicked his way into the text message.

Forget coffee, it said. *Make it dinner and you're on.*

THIRTEEN

Carolina had always loved Italian restaurants. She loved the food, she loved the wine, she loved the atmosphere. Whenever she had a choice of where to dine, she would choose Italian without a second thought, and had a stable of favorite eateries around the city where she made her regular rounds.

Tonight, however, she noticed none of it. Her lasagna lay on her plate, cold and congealing; her glass of red wine sat nearly untouched. Around her, the wait staff milled and the other customers chatted and laughed, but all she could see or hear was the man sitting across the table from her. In fact, she couldn't take her eyes off of him.

"Do you come here often?" Michael asked her, smirking at the clichéd question.

She shook her head slowly. "Never been here, actually. A little out of the way for me. I usually stay in the city." She had actually chosen this restaurant because it was on the outskirts of town, and she was less likely to run into anyone there she might know.

A sign that you shouldn't be doing this, maybe, she chided herself, but then shook off the thought. She couldn't have *not* done it. She'd thought about saying "no" to the invitation, but in the end she'd just had to find out—

"You?" she asked, cutting off her own thoughts before they got the best of her.

He shook his head as well, then picked up his fork and pushed his food around on his plate—linguini with clam sauce, also without a bite taken out of it. She watched his long fingers gripping the utensil, imagined them writing out a prescription or patting a patient's hand reassuringly. She also remembered the handshake they had shared at the fundraising dinner and the cool, soft feeling of his skin.

"I don't go out to eat much," he said, looking back up at her. "My wife's a little on the frugal side, so we stay home a lot."

Carolina was sure she heard a note of sadness in his voice when he said that, but she tried not to linger on it. She didn't really know this man and certainly didn't know his wife, and she didn't want to speculate about their relationship. Didn't want to think about what she was doing there. Definitely didn't want to think about where this all was going.

"So, tell me about your practice," she said, again trying to derail her train of thought. "How long have you worked there?"

"Oh, about ten years now," Michael replied, sitting back in his chair and looking a little relieved to be on a different topic. "I've been friends with Scott, my partner, since med school. We always wanted to work together but never had a chance until then."

"Where did you work before this?" Carolina picked up her glass of wine and took a sip—no sense in letting a good drink go to waste, she figured. Rolling the tart liquid around in her mouth, she tried to keep her mind focused on the current conversation.

Michael laughed a little. "Actually, I was an ER doctor."

Carolina smiled. "Really?"

"Yeah, really. It was—well, it was exciting, I have to admit, especially compared to what I do now. There's a big difference between, you know, tending to twenty bus accident victims at once and making sure that elderly widows get their flu shots on time."

Feeling a blush in her cheeks—*Happens every time,* she thought, eyeing the wine—Carolina put down her glass and looked at Michael again. She pictured him in a white coat and scrubs, stethoscope around his neck, running into an emergency examination area to administer to a seriously injured patient. "That must have been an interesting job. Rewarding, though, right?"

Michael nodded, smiling a bit sheepishly. "It was. I did love it." He looked to the right for a moment, his eyes absently searching the room as he thought. Looking back at Carolina, he shrugged. "But, you know, you grow older and you have a family to support... Honestly, I didn't want to go into private practice at first. Thought it would be too boring, too stifling. But I've come to love it, too. My patients are truly priceless, and there's something to be said for routine and stability."

Sitting back in her chair as well, Carolina sighed. Routine and stability... Were they really all that great? She thought about David for a moment, still on his business trip. She pictured him sitting in a meeting in Colorado, going back to his hotel afterward and ordering room service. Calling his wife and kids before bed. Sleeping, getting up in the morning to do it all over again.

And what would she be doing just then, if Michael hadn't sent her that text message? Cleaning up the dinner dishes, making sure the kids did their homework, probably doing some work she'd brought home as well. Before bed she would take a shower, then lay out her clothes for the next morning. She would set her alarm for six o'clock; she would sleep on the left side of the bed.

"I think that routine can sometimes lull a person into apathy," she said before she even knew the words had left her mouth.

Pausing with his wine glass in his hands, Michael simply looked at her, his brows lowered. Returning his gaze, she put her fingers up to touch her lips lightly. "Sorry," she said. "I have this bad habit of saying things before I think."

He put his glass down. "Well, it was a little blunt, but you're right."

For a few moments, there was silence at the table, while the restaurant continued to buzz around them. Carolina blinked her eyes slowly, looking a Michael, still trying to make sense of what she was doing there.

"The charity stuff," she finally said, her voice distant and her mind about a million miles away. "We should talk about that."

Across from her, Michael pushed his plate back and leaned his arms on the table, folded in front of him. He looked at her just as intently as she stared at him, obviously feeling just as Carolina did: as though there were something more there between them than either could see with their eyes.

"We should," he agreed, narrowing his eyes at her as if coming to some conclusion inside of his head. "But do you really think we're going to?"

The blush rose with renewed fervor in Carolina's cheeks. She looked down at her lap, a little flustered by his forthrightness.

"Seriously," he went on. "That's not why we're here, is it?"

Looking back up at Michael, Carolina leaned forward as well, resting her arms on the table just as he did. Feeling emboldened, she held his gaze once more, and felt a sort of—well, it felt strange to realize it, but a sort of trancelike sensation when she looked into his eyes. There was still something about him that seemed so familiar, something about the way he looked at her that made her feel like they'd known each other forever.

"Why *are* we here?" she asked, her voice low.

He shrugged, a disarmingly nonchalant gesture given the weightiness of the discussion. Carolina expected him to smile, but he didn't. "I'm not sure," he said, reaching for his wine again. He downed what remained in the glass. "I can't really explain it. I felt somewhat compelled by you—you're so beautiful. Since the first moment I met you I've felt like there's…*something* between us. Like we're…" He laughed, unsure if he should even say it. "Like we're meant to be together. I can't explain it."

For a moment, Michael slid his hand across the table toward her, as if he were reaching out to touch her. But then he pulled his hand back. He sat up straighter; he stared deeply into her eyes. For a moment, Carolina thought he was speechless—as she was herself. But then he spoke once more.

"So, when can I see you again?"

FOURTEEN

"You're crazy, Carolina. What are you doing here?"

Checking her makeup in the mirror on the back of the sun visor, she sighed.

"See? Talking to yourself. An obvious sign of psychosis."

Flipping the visor back up, she looked across the nearly empty parking lot ahead of her, at the restaurant near the water. A seafood place—not her first choice, but the location was right and, besides, she'd chosen the restaurant last time.

"What are you doing here?" she repeated, her voice a murmur, her mind far away. She was thinking of Michael, of his face, his smile, his hands, just as she had so many times in the last week since they'd met up for dinner. At the most inopportune times—while listening to her husband talk about his day at work; while stopped in traffic on the way to pick the kids up from school—she'd been accosted by these memories, these feelings that she knew she shouldn't be having.

But she couldn't help it. She didn't want to find Michael so intriguing. Something—a force that she couldn't explain—was compelling her to follow him.

Sighing again, she grabbed her purse and threw open the door of her black SUV. As she stepped out, she felt a chill from the cool breeze that blew in off the bay. Reaching back into the car, she grabbed her gray trench coat and hurriedly put it on, cinching the belt tightly around her small waist. Still standing by the side of the car, she shoved her hand in her pocket—and felt her cell phone frantically vibrating.

Withdrawing it and flipping it open, the screen told her she had a new text message.

Carolina, it read. *Where are you? Can't wait to see you. M.*

He'd been sending her messages like this all week—saying that he wanted to see her, he wanted to talk to her, he couldn't stop thinking about her. Sometimes she had answered him; sometimes she hadn't. On the whole, she just didn't really know what to do about him. About this situation.

Still, there she was. Standing outside this restaurant. While he was inside it, text messaging her, wondering where she was.

Closing the phone, she slid it back into her pocket and just stood there for a moment, looking at the building.

"Alright, I'm going!" she shouted into the wind, then ran across the parking lot, her high heels clacking against the asphalt.

***

An hour and a half later, Carolina was feeling much warmer, much happier and much more relaxed. In fact, she was wondering what all that hesitation in the parking lot had been about.

"And so I told him," Michael was saying, trying to keep from laughing, "that if he *ever* did that to his sister again, he'd be grounded for life."

Carolina smirked, enjoying the conversation. "I've heard those exact same words come out of my own mouth," she admitted. "I hate grounding them. But I end up doing it the most. My husband—" She stopped at this word and just looked at Michael as it hung there between them. "Well," she went on, fidgeting a little in her chair, "we're kind of good cop/bad cop. And guess who gets to be the bad cop most of the time."

Michael was silent for a moment, sitting with his hands folded on the table in front of him. He looked at Carolina intently, his smile growing slightly fainter. "I think I have the opposite problem," he replied. "I'm always the good guy. My wife, Julie—" He paused, too, at the mention of his significant other. He looked down at the white tablecloth, traced a wrinkle on it with the tip of his finger. Thinking that he was lost in a little internal conflict—and knowing exactly what that felt like—Carolina gave him a moment.

"She's a bit high-strung," he continued, finally coming back to her. "Doesn't like to give our children too much leeway." He shrugged, a resigned and sort of sad look on his face. "I feel bad for them sometimes, so I probably let them get away with more than I should. It's not the best parenting method, I know."

Sitting forward, Carolina picked up a forkful of seared tuna and took a bite, slowly chewing as she thought. "Are you happy in your marriage?" she asked when she was done, sitting back and looking at him intently. He seemed taken aback by the question, so she added, "Sorry, I can be a little blunt sometimes. Comes from running a business."

He smiled at her, though, and sat back in his chair as well, shaking off the unexpected inquiry. Actually, he looked relaxed, happy to be there—and especially happy to be sitting across from her.

"No problem," he said. "Nothing wrong with being honest." He turned his head for a moment and looked out the nearby window at the boats on the bay, his brow lowered as he pondered his answer. In profile, Carolina noticed, he was even more handsome: a little brooding, a little more intense. The muscles in his jaw flexed and released as he thought. The corner of his mouth twisted up in an unconscious tic, a sign of the ideas working their way through his mind.

Carolina shifted again in her seat as she watched him think, willing herself not to find this man attractive.

"You know," he began after a few more moments, turning his gaze back to Carolina. She smiled as he faced her fully, unable to restrain herself. He paused and smiled back. "What is it?"

Carolina blushed a little, fearing she'd been caught admiring him. "Nothing," she said. "Go on."

Michael waited a moment more, his smile turning into a smirk as if he knew what she'd been thinking. "Anyway," he finally said, still staring at her. "I was going to say that yes, I am happy in my marriage. In some ways. And in some ways I'm not."

Carolina picked up her fork again and poked at her fish, now grown cold and looking fairly unappetizing. "Well, that's honesty for you," she said with a small laugh. She looked back up at Michael. "But I guess I could say the same. I love my children, and I have a good life. I'm proud of what David and I have built together. But some days..."

Her sentence drifted off into the low hum of the restaurant. Around them, a few other patrons, scattered around the dining room, carried on their low-volume conversations. Nearby, a waiter refilled salt and pepper shakers in an empty booth. Near the doorway, two young, female greeters awaited a lunch crowd that just wasn't coming. Carolina wondered how Michael had even found this place—a question she would ask him some other time.

"Some days it's just not enough?" he finished for her, his voice soft. She looked up at him, into his eyes, and for the first time, she didn't feel nervous. Gazing at him now, she felt like he completely understood her, like she didn't have to explain the longing she'd felt for so long—for something more than the life she had was able to offer her.

"I feel awful about it," she said, feeling the sudden pressure of tears at the corners of her eyes. She looked down at her lap, almost embarrassed to be admitting all this to a stranger but at the same time, so relieved to have someone to say it to. "But I just don't love him anymore. I care about him, and I'm committed to our life together, but—"

"But you have to take care of yourself, too." Across the table, Michael's face was placid, serene, his tone so completely sympathetic.

Carolina nodded in response. "I have my business, and I have my friends. I can do whatever I like. I have a lot of freedom. I can't really complain about my life at all. But emotionally…" She shook her head and held her hands up as if in surrender. "It's just not there. Do you know what I mean?"

Michael smiled at her again. "I know exactly what you mean," he replied. "My life is perfect, too. Good family, great career, perfect health. So, why am I always so unhappy?"

Once again, as he had at their last meeting, Michael slid a hand across the table toward Carolina. This time, however, he let himself make contact, his fingers moving easily onto the top of her hand where it lay next to her plate. He looked relieved when Carolina did not move away.

For a moment they both simply looked at their hands, at this union that was at once so innocent and so full of meaning.

"All I know, Carolina, is that I've felt happier since I've met you." She did not look up at him, so he continued. "I feel like I have something to look forward to, something to aspire to, even though I'm not quite sure what it is yet. All I know is that I'm drawn to you. I feel like there's something bigger than us at work here."

Carolina laughed lightly again. "What, like fate or something?" Her tone came out a little more sarcastically than she'd meant it to, but she was feeling so confused, she couldn't help it. She still watched their hands. She wanted to pull hers away, but at the same time she wanted to leave it.

"Maybe," Michael replied, obviously not seeing it as a joke. "I can't explain it. But I can't help feeling like you and I, Carolina, want the same things out of life."

She looked up at him. "And what *do* you want out of life?"

He answered quickly. "Happiness. Peace of mind. A good life with a woman who understands me inside and out."

Carolina looked down at their hands again, thinking for a moment. "You don't have those things now?" she asked him.

"Not yet. But I have a feeling they will come to me."

***

"Carolina, what have you done?"

Flicking on the turn signal, she made a quick right into downtown traffic, heading south, back toward her office. Glancing at the console to check the time, she saw that she'd been out to lunch for almost three hours.

Well, that's the least of your worries now, she told herself, merging in between two delivery trucks and glancing in the rearview mirror nervously, as if paranoid that someone were following her.

As the flow of vehicles came to a halt at a traffic light, she closed her eyes and leaned her head back against the rest on the top of her seat. Immediately, images began to flood her mind: Michael's smile, his hand on top of hers. The way he said her name, softly and slowly like a meditation. The butterflies in her stomach when he looked at her so longingly.

The soft touch of his lips as he'd kissed her goodbye.

Sighing, Carolina recalled the cool breeze on her cheeks as they'd stood outside the restaurant, next to her car, looking out over the water. She'd sensed that Michael had been stalling, that he hadn't wanted to leave, though she hadn't known why.

"I really have to get back to work," she'd said almost apologetically as she'd reached into her purse for her keys. And then, in one deft motion, he'd put an arm around her and swept her close to him. Before she'd known what was happening, he'd been kissing her, and the entire world had dropped out around her. No more car, no more asphalt, no more boats; the wind had ceased and there was nothing but his strong arms around her, his mouth on hers. The connection between their bodies had been electric. Whatever reservations she'd had, that moment had obliterated them. She hadn't been able to keep herself from kissing him back.

"Carolina!" she said again, a bit of panic creeping into her voice. Her hands gripped the steering wheel in front of her. "What are you *doing?*"

In the pocket of her trench coat, her cell phone buzzed to life, startling her out of her thoughts. She jumped a bit and opened her eyes, then dug quickly into her pocket to retrieve the vibrating phone. Flipping it open, she found another new text message.

It is fate, it read. *I can feel it. Can you? Counting the minutes until I can see you again... M.*

Behind her, a car horn blared. She looked up and saw that the light had turned green. Closing the phone and dropping it onto her lap, she put her foot down hard on the gas pedal and the SUV tore away, carrying her into the future and whatever awaited her there.

FIFTEEN

Dear Carolina,

I can't begin to explain how I feel about you right now. My feelings evolve each day that I know you. With every moment, I am more drawn to you. My thoughts are consumed by your face, your skin, the sound of your voice.

Carolina, you are beautiful inside and out. I cannot imagine my life without you in it now. You are the missing piece of my puzzle, I am sure of it.

—M.

"Mom, we gotta go!"

Hearing the sound of her son's voice calling to her from out in the kitchen, Carolina quickly clicked the email closed. "Be right there, Patrick," she shouted back, though she did not move from her seat. She needed a moment to compose herself.

In the few weeks since they had met up at that seafood restaurant for lunch, Michael had been sending her messages like this every day—letters about how much he missed her, how much he thought about her, how compelled he was to see her again. They hadn't gotten together again yet—hadn't been able to find time away from their families—but Carolina knew that it was just a matter of time.

Don't want to rush anything, she thought absently, her mind drifting to an image of Michael's broad smile, the gleam in his eyes as he looked at her. *But then again...*

"Mom!" In the kitchen, her children were ready and waiting on her to drive them to school. She had been letting Patrick play the chauffeur more and more lately, but today she would be done with work early and wanted to pick them all up herself. Figured she would take them shopping, have a little quality time, just the four of them, while David spent another evening at his office.

"Coming!" she called, then stood up from her chair and straightened her suit. Running her fingers through her hair, she looked out the window: another sunny, gorgeous day. She wondered if Michael was out there somewhere on his bike, enjoying the fresh air. Over lunch that last time he'd told her all about his love of the sport, about his early morning rides. The very next day, he'd started texting her pictures of the scenery he saw along the way.

Remembering this, she pulled her cell phone out of her jacket pocket and quickly flipped it open. "Download, download!" she muttered to it as she waited for the new picture message to come in.

"*Mom!*" Patrick's calls were getting frantic. She could hear him sighing loudly as the girls bickered with one another—all the usual noise of a busy morning.

"Coming!" she called back again, glancing out into the hallway to make sure that no one was coming. On her phone's small screen, the picture finally came into view: Michael's face in front of an expanse of blue sky, snow-capped Mt. Rainier in the distant background. He wore a black helmet and orange-tinted sunglasses; his cheeks were red, and the ends of his hair stuck to his damp neck. He looked tired…but he was smiling like the happiest man on earth.

Carolina swiped a finger across the screen, as if she could reach out and touch him, could wipe the sweat from his brow.

"We'll be in the car, Mom," Patrick shouted, and then Carolina heard the door to the garage open and slam shut.

Lingering on the picture on her phone, she smiled wanly. "Be right there," she said softly, absently, as she flipped the phone closed. There would be plenty of time to look at it again later. For now, her life was calling.

***

Michael,

    I keep looking at the picture you sent me from your bike ride this morning. I'm drawn to your face over and over again. Something about your smile is so familiar, so comforting to me. If I go too long without seeing it, I feel as though I'm missing something, some important part of my own being.

    Before the night I met you, I never would have guessed that I could feel like this. I still can't explain it or even really understand it.

    But now, I don't know how I'll get through another day without seeing you.

Carolina

Leaning back against the counter in exam room one, Michael stared at the cell phone in his hands, at Carolina's words laid out on its screen. Judging by the time stamp, she'd emailed him just before she'd gone into work. He pictured her sitting in her SUV, tapping out this message and sending it off before heading into the office. He'd missed it when it had come in; he'd been with a patient.

Running a hand through his hair, he shook his head a little, trying to get rid of the fuzzy, dazed feeling that had come over him, but he could not take his eyes off of those words. *Don't know how I'll get through another day without seeing you,* he read again silently, a pang shooting through his chest. Raising his eyes and staring blankly at the far wall, at the cabinets full of medication samples and tongue depressors, he wondered when he *would* get to see her again.

"Not soon enough," he said quietly, but the thought was interrupted by two quick raps on the exam room door.

"Dr. Sanford?" called Marissa, his assistant. "Your next patient is here."

Standing up straight, he slipped the phone back into the pocket of his white coat. "Concentrate, concentrate," he told himself, then blew out a strong, quick breath to help himself focus. As the door opened, he smiled at Marissa and the elderly woman standing next to her.

"Mrs. Hamilton," he said. "Back again so soon? What can I do for you today?"

Helping the patient up onto the exam table, he spoke to her gently and inquired about her condition, then set about a physical exam. It seemed that her cold symptoms hadn't abated since she'd been in the office several weeks earlier, and Michael was a little concerned that she could have been developing pneumonia—always a possibility with his elderly patients.

"How would you feel about going into the hospital overnight so I can monitor you?" he asked her, sitting down on a stool next to the table so as not to tower over her.

"Well, if you think it's for the best," Mrs. Hamilton replied. "I don't like hospitals, but I trust you with my life, Dr. Sanford. If you say I should do it, then I'll do it!"

Assisting the older woman down from the table once more, Michael escorted her back out to the reception area and left her in the care of Marissa, who would help her arrange the hospital admission. Leaning over Marissa's desk, he checked his schedule quickly and saw that he had another fifteen minutes before his next patient was due to arrive.

Just enough, he thought, making a fast retreat to his office.

Once inside, he closed the door and made his way over to the desk, where he sat down on his creaky, old chair. Leaning back, he reached his arms up in the air, cell phone already clutched in one hand, stretching as he thought of what to write.

'I miss you,' he thought. *No, too obvious. 'I want you.' No, too forward. 'I...'*

As the inspiration hit him, he brought his arms back down and flipped open the phone. He clicked his way into its email program and drew up a new, blank message.

I have to see you, he read silently to himself as he wrote. *Tonight. Eight o'clock, at the—*

Jolted by the ringing of the phone on his desk, Michael jumped almost right out of his chair. Putting a hand up to his chest as if it could still his thumping heart, he simply glared at the phone for a moment, its shrill, electronic ringtone reverberating in the otherwise silent room. Leaning over the desk, he reached for the receiver and grabbed it roughly, then brought it up to his ear.

"Yes, Dr. Sanford," he said, his tone gruff.

"Daddy?" came the bright, cheery reply.

Michael squeezed his eyes shut, his face twisting into a grimace. "Hi, Emily. Sorry about sounding so mean. You caught me in the middle of—of some work stuff, sweetheart. What's going on?"

"I'm in between classes," the girl went on quickly, "so I've only got a minute, but I was thinking, do you have any plans for tonight?"

Pausing, Michael brought his other hand up and looked at his still-open cell phone.

I have to see you, he read, feeling a knot forming in the pit of his stomach. His eyes lingered over the words, Carolina's face flashing through his mind and a rush of emotion—longing, disappointment, guilt—passing through his body. He forced himself to snap the phone closed, and then tossed it onto the desk.

"No, sweetheart," he said to his daughter, his tone even and gentle. "But I'd love to do something with you. What do you have in mind?"

***

"Mom, I love my new shoes." Alexis did a little jump and spin, full of energy as only a twelve-year-old could be. She landed roughly on the aforementioned footwear, then kicked her foot out in front of her to look at it.

"Good, sweetheart," Carolina replied, absently putting her hand on Alexis' shoulder as she talked to the maitre d'. "Four, please, and we have one more coming in about half an hour."

"Mom, are you sure Dad'll be here?" Lindsay asked, not bothering to take her eyes off of her cell phone, where she was busy texting one of her seemingly millions of friends. Glancing at her, Carolina put a hand to her coat pocket, making sure that her own cell phone was there—and not in the hands of one of her curious children. She made a mental note to erase her messages and pictures as soon as she could get a minute alone.

"I'm sure," she told her oldest daughter, reaching over to push a lock of hair out of her eyes. Lindsay glanced up at her and smiled quickly, but then returned to her phone and her all-important texting. "How about you put that away so we can have a nice dinner together?"

Lindsay continued typing for a moment, but then hit the "send" button and slid the phone into the back pocket of her jeans. She smiled at her mother one more time. "Done and done," she said, then turned her attention to making a fuss over Alexis' shoes. Carolina watched them interacting and said a brief thanks that she'd been blessed with such polite, considerate and just plain *nice* children.

"Right this way, ma'am," the maitre d' said to her then, interrupting her thoughts. Corralling the girls and shooing them on in front of her into the restaurant, Carolina glanced outside and saw Patrick in the SUV across the street. She'd given him car-parking duties while she'd gone in with the girls to get a table.

He'll find us, she thought, then turned to follow the girls through the maze of the dining room.

It wasn't quite eight o'clock yet, but for a weeknight, the place was already quite busy. This was a pretty popular family restaurant in the heart of the city; Carolina often brought the kids there and sometimes even had to wait to get a table. They'd been lucky tonight and gotten seated within only a few minutes of their arrival.

"Mmm, that smells *good!*" Alexis said loudly as they passed by a table full of adults and children, all of them with plates full of food in front of them. "Mom, can I get a cheeseburger?" She stopped and turned around toward Carolina, her eyebrows raised in expectation, her hands clasped in front of her as if she were pleading.

Busy with a new incoming text message on her phone, Lindsay did not see that her little sister had stopped so

abruptly and crashed right into her, practically knocking her
to the floor.

"Hey, watch it!" Alexis nearly shouted, rubbing her
elbow where she'd bumped it on somebody's chair.

"Lindsay, phone away, now," Carolina told her oldest
daughter calmly but firmly as she reached out to inspect
Alexis' injury. Bending over, she kissed it through the young
girl's sweater. "I think you'll live."

"Can I still have a cheeseburger?" Alexis replied, a
wide grin spreading across her face.

"Yes, you may," Carolina replied, smiling warmly as
she pinched the girl quickly on the chin.

In front of the group, the maitre d' had disappeared
somewhere; standing up straight again, Carolina peered
around the room, trying to find him. Scanning the crowd, she
looked for his telltale white shirt and black tie, but found—

"Oh, my God," she whispered, her hand going
involuntarily to cover her mouth.

"Mom, what is it?" Alexis asked, once again prancing
around, her eyes back on her new shoes.

"It's, uh," Carolina stammered as she reached out a
hand to still her daughter, her eyes locked on a table across
the room. "It's, uh, nothing," she finally replied.

Alexis turned her head in the same direction. "What's
over there?"

"Nothing," Carolina answered shortly, putting a hand
on Alexis' head and turning it back the other way.

But it wasn't nothing... It was Michael. Just sitting
there at a table with his wife and his son and his daughter. As
the others all ate and talked around him, he simply sat back
in his chair, one hand on his lap, the other gripping the stem
of a wine glass on the table. And he stared at her. At
Carolina. His eyes locked on her as if he'd been watching
her the whole time, a serene half smile playing on his lips.

The girls, she thought. He must have heard the commotion they'd caused; it must have drawn his attention.

"Do you see the maitre d', sweetheart?" she asked Alexis, trying to spin her around to face the other side of the room.

"There he is, Mom!" Alexis shouted, spying the maitre d' near a table over toward the left. She grabbed Lindsay's hand and began to skip off, but then turned back and took Carolina's hand as well. "Come on, Mom," she said, tugging her away. Reluctantly, with only a last sidelong glance over at Michael, Carolina allowed herself to go.

"Five places, madam," the maitre d' announced as they arrived at the table, "for your late guest." He presented the table with a flourish of his arm and then went around and pulled the chairs out for the girls, who giggled as they took their seats.

"Thank you," Carolina mumbled, dropping herself down onto a chair wearily and grabbing the nearest glass of water. She downed half of it, then propped her elbows on the table and rested her face in her hands. Her cheeks were burning, her mind racing a mile a minute.

What am I going to do? she thought. *We can't both be here. We can't be seen together. What if he comes over and says something to me? What if the kids get suspicious? Oh, God, what if David—*

Snapping her head to attention, she shoved her hand into her jacket pocket and grabbed her vibrating cell phone.

Don't worry, the text message read. *Don't be afraid. Wish I could be with you. Will be soon. I think I'm falling in love with you. M.*

Sixteen

Normally, Carolina loved presentations. Though she was the head of the company, she often ran them herself—got right in and pitched campaigns to their clients alongside her staff. She'd been in advertising for so long, it was like a second language to her, but the ideas and innovations she came up with were still always fresh and exciting. As far as a career went, nothing could have made her happier, and she truly enjoyed every minute she spent at her office.

But all that changed when she met Michael. Since then, she just hadn't been able to concentrate on anything else.

What are you doing? she typed into her cell phone, then hit the "send" button. She turned her attention back to the front of the conference room, where Allison, one of her female employees, gestured cheerily to a blow-up of a pie chart.

Within moments, the answer came in. Carolina had turned the ringer and the vibration off on her phone, so as not to disrupt the meeting in any way, but still she'd clutched it in her hand so she could see the screen blinking when a message arrived.

Thinking about you, it read. *Have I mentioned that I'm becoming a little obsessed with you?*

"Hm, only a thousand or so times," Carolina muttered quietly to herself, a hint of a smile playing on her lips. She looked up and around quickly to make sure no one had heard her. All the meeting attendees—the suits from a pretty prestigious health and beauty company in the city—were enraptured by Allison's facts and figures. Carolina looked back to her phone.

Gotta admit, I can't stop thinking about you either, she replied. *But you knew that already.*

In the month and a half since they'd first met, Carolina and Michael had gotten together a handful of times—for dinner, for lunch, for coffee at an out-of-the-way café on the outskirts of the city. They'd sat on park benches shaded by great, overhanging tree boughs and looked into each other's eyes for what had seemed like hours on end; they'd huddled in the backseat of Carolina's SUV, arms around one another, confessing all their hopes and dreams and desires. They had kissed; they had touched. They had held hands like it was the most meaningful contact on earth. And in a way, it was. These little moments were all that they had, and she treasured every second of them.

But still…

I'm tired of hiding, she typed out impulsively, then sent it off before she could think about it. She set her phone down on the table, turned back to Allison and tried to catch up with the presentation. She had supervised this project from the beginning and had been so pleased with the way it had turned out, and she knew she should have shown more interest in how the clients were reacting to it. This was her company, after all, her employee, her pitch. She shouldn't have been slipping so far off her game.

But she couldn't help it. She couldn't think of anything but Michael.

Picking up the phone again, she flipped it open. *Where are you?* she typed and sent quickly, beginning to feel irritated that he hadn't answered her yet. She pictured him at work, wearing his white coat, leaning over a patient and talking to them in that calming, soothing voice of his. Then she imagined that *she* was the patient, sitting on his exam table, his strong hands on her back, running the cold stethoscope smoothly across her bare skin and listening as she breathed deeply in and out…

In her hand, the phone's screen lit up. She clicked into the new text message.

Sorry. At home today—day off—but had a call from the hospital. Elderly patient with pneumonia.

Carolina sighed, relieved that it had only been something work related that had kept him from answering. *It's okay,* she replied. *Sorry to be pushy. I'm just thinking too much today.*

At the front of the room, Allison was passing around packets of information—demographics, pricing, the works. This was a big client and a fairly important account, but Carolina had confidence that they would win the contract. She watched as the executives sipped their coffee and perused the information.

The cell phone blinked. *As long as you're thinking about me,* the new message read. *Because I've been thinking about you since the moment I woke up this morning. You're so beautiful. I wish I could see your face right now.*

Sitting back in her chair, Carolina looked out the conference room window, at the skyline of the city stretching out in all directions. She closed her eyes for a moment, trying to calm the storm clouds that were thundering through her mind. "Concentrate," she said to herself quietly. "Concentrate."

But how could she be expected to do that when she had a man like Michael in her life?

In her hand, the cell phone blinked to life once more. *Are you at work?* his next message read.

Yes, and in a meeting, she replied, *though I'm having a lot of trouble paying attention. You have no idea what effect you have on me.*

Somewhere out there, Carolina mused, her children were walking around the halls of their school. Her husband was in a high-rise, probably running his own meeting—something about takeovers or mergers, some sort of big-money deal. All sorts of people were out on the streets, just living their lives. Working. Playing. Being happy. Each of them following their own routine, chasing after their own dream.

And there she was, stuck in a conference room instead of following where her heart longed to take her.

The phone blinked. *Can you get away?*

Instinctively, Carolina smiled again, but brought a hand up to her mouth to cover it. Looking around the room once more, she hoped that it wasn't too obvious to anyone else what she'd been doing. As the head of the company, she, of course, had the leeway to take calls and messages during meetings; it wasn't unheard of for her to communicate with clients or coworkers while one of her staff had the floor. But this—well, if anyone knew who she was messaging this time, it would be a scandal, a bombshell, just the worst thing that could have happened to her. She'd spent years building up a reputation as a strong entrepreneur, an ethical boss, an admirable and enviable player in the Seattle business scene. She wasn't the sort of person who did things like this—who blew off meetings and let herself get preoccupied by daydreams.

But…this was Michael, she told herself. And when it came to him, she was finding out, she really had no choice in the matter.

Yes, she replied. *Chateau Deneuve. Meet me in an hour.*

SEVENTEEN

"And how did you say you know this place again?" Michael asked, examining the gilt mirror frame above the dressing table. He'd never been to Chateau Deneuve before—had never had reason to. He'd driven past it a million times, had seen it off the highway leading out of the city that he took home from work every day. It was a huge, hulking, sort of castle-like structure; he'd never had any idea it would be so posh on the inside.

He turned to look at Carolina, who was hanging on to a corner of the sofa—deep-brown suede cushions, an array of velvet pillows arranged across it—with one hand and reaching down to take off her high heels with the other.

"They're a client," she replied, standing now in her bare feet on the thick, gold rug that delineated the lounge area of the suite. She dug her toes into it and then kicked her shoes off to one side. "Did a campaign for them a couple years ago. The owner loved my work so much, he said I could stay for free whenever I want."

Michael smirked, now running his fingertips along a cream-colored silk lampshade. "And how often do you take him up on this offer?"

Laughing, Carolina sat down on the sofa, its enormous cushions enveloping her petite frame. She held out her hands at her sides, palms upturned. "First time," she said, then laughed once more.

Pausing outside the bathroom door, Michael leaned inside and flicked on the light switch. Everything inside the enormous room was pristine, sparkling, and created for the sole purpose of comfort—an enormous Jacuzzi, candles waiting to be lit, fluffy, white bathrobes hanging from gold hooks on the wall. Letting out a low whistle of appreciation, he turned the light off and withdrew.

On the sofa, Carolina had stretched out her long, thin, beautifully toned legs. She was wearing a black wrap dress, low cut and perfectly fitted to her figure, and a collection of gold necklaces—some beaded, some chains, an eclectic mix. On her ears were diamonds. Her lips were painted red, her blond hair flowing free.

"First time for everything, huh?" he asked her, his voice low and husky. He leaned his shoulder against the wall and just looked at her, marveling at how relaxed she looked. Reaching for his wedding ring to twist it around and around his finger—a nervous habit, a subconscious tic he employed whenever he was feeling uneasy—he stopped himself, and instead shoved his hands in the pockets of his pants.

"You look nice today," he offered, but then laughed at himself. He sounded like a teenage boy talking to a girl he had a crush on. He wondered why he could send her a thousand text messages detailing all the aspects of her beauty, but saying the words aloud left him tripping on his own tongue.

"Why don't you come sit down?" Carolina replied gently, cocking her head to one side and patting the sofa, as if sensing how anxious he was.

After considering the invitation for only a moment, Michael made his way across the spacious suite and over to where Carolina sat. He settled himself gently at the end of the sofa, just past her bare feet. Instinctually, he reached out and took them in his hands and rested her heels on his lap.

"I don't know how you wear those shoes all the time," he said, pressing his thumbs into her arches and moving them in slow, deep circles. He glanced up at Carolina. Her head rested back against the arm of the sofa; her eyes were closed, her lips slightly parted. "They can't be good for your feet," he added, staring at her. "Medically, I mean." He continued rubbing, working his way down to her heels then back up to her toes. "You've got to take care of your feet. Something happens to them, what are you going to walk on?"

Eyes still closed, Carolina laughed, a low, seductive sound that barely left her throat. "Thank you for the assessment, doctor. Do you think we'll have to amputate?"

Clearing his throat and trying to keep a straight face, Michael raised one eyebrow dramatically. "Well, ma'am, let's see," he began, making his voice theatrically deep. "I think…"

Without missing a beat, he laid his hands flat against the tops of her feet and slid them slowly up to her ankles, to her calves, his thumbs running along the insides. "I think," he said again, looking down at her legs, his hands gently massaging her smooth, pale skin, his fingertips venturing up closer to her knees. "I think that you'll probably be okay. But I might have to examine you more, uh, *in depth* to get a better diagnosis."

Raising her head, Carolina looked at him, the most enigmatic smile on her lips. "Michael," she said softly, reaching out a hand to touch his hair, his face.

Michael raised his head to look back at her, and their eyes locked. "Carolina," he replied, and then they just sat there in silence for a while, looking at one another. As the sun struggled to shine in through the window's thick drapery, as people passed by in the hallway, talking loudly, as cars far out on the freeway revved their engines and sped to their destinations, in this hotel room, time stood still. To Michael, there was no one in the world at that moment but the two of them, nothing else that mattered except their connection. He could have sat there with her forever, just looking in her eyes.

"Michael," she said again, curling her legs back up beneath her, inching her way closer to him on the sofa. "What are we doing here?"

The question startled Michael, but he did not look away from her. He shrugged. And then he smiled. "Having a nice afternoon together?" he asked, trying to keep it lighthearted even though—or perhaps because—he knew what she meant by it, was aware of all the implications of what she had said. What were they doing together, at a hotel, in the middle of the day? What about their responsibilities, their families, their spouses? The lives they'd each built over years and years and years, the histories they had apart from one other? Did none of that matter? Or could they really put it all aside and just be together, just do what their hearts compelled them to do?

I can, he thought. Looking deeply into Carolina's eyes, moving his hand up to her bare thigh, leaning in closer, he was more sure of that one fact than ever.

"I don't know what we're doing here," he admitted. "I just know that I have to be with you." He paused for a moment, not sure if he should say what he really wanted to—but then he just couldn't hold back any longer. The feeling was much too strong to keep to himself.

"Carolina, we're soul mates, you and I," he told her, pulling her close and wrapping his arms around her. For a moment, her body stiffened, as if she were shocked by what he'd said, but then she softened and melted into his arms.

Laying her head on his shoulder, she inched in as close to him as she possibly could, until nothing but their clothing separated them. Her closeness gave Michael the confidence he needed to go on.

"I've never felt this way with anyone before," he said, running a hand slowly over her hair as he spoke. "I feel...*complete* when I'm with you. Like I've been missing something my whole life and haven't even known it—and that something is you."

Pulling away from her a bit, he put a hand on her chin and raised her face to look at him. Peering deep into her eyes, he told her, "I love you, Carolina."

And then he kissed her, roughly and passionately, like a man who was tasting water after a thousand years in the desert. He closed his arms tightly around her, as if he could make their bodies become one, as if they could simply melt into one another.

"Carolina," he whispered, pulling his head back so he could look into her eyes once again. They were like a drug to him; he always needed more.

"Michael," she replied breathlessly, her lips flushed. She put a hand up to his face and smiled at him. "I love you, too," she whispered, her eyes growing slightly moist. "God, it's such a relief to finally say it. And to know that you feel exactly the same way I do."

Leaning in again, Michael kissed her on the forehead, slipping a hand inside the shoulder of her dress at the same time. He rested his palm on the base of her neck, his thumb tracing the outline of her collarbone. Closing his eyes for a moment, taking in the sensation of her skin against his lips and the scent of her flowery perfume—lilacs, he thought—he felt their connection, the bond between them that he knew now could never be broken.

"I love you, too," she whispered again, and then broke away from him. Standing up slowly, she took his hand and led him over to the bed.

Eighteen

Carolina was up with the sun on most mornings, but it had been a while since she'd felt such a spring in her step. Jumping out of bed, she threw wide the curtains and felt a smile on her face that could not be restrained, an energy in her spirit that she hoped would last.

Looking back toward the bed, however, she felt herself deflate just the slightest bit. On her side, the sheets and blanket lay unmade, disheveled by sleep. On her husband's side, everything was still tucked in and perfect, looking like it had been untouched for some time.

"That's because it has been," she muttered, slouching back over to her side of the bed and pulling the covers up neatly. With a sigh, she picked up her pillow and plumped it, then shoved it underneath the top of the duvet. She couldn't remember the last time she and David had slept in the same bed together.

"Well," she said, heading over toward her dresser, tugging off her nightshirt as she went. "That's what you get for marrying a successful businessman." She spoke loudly, just to convince herself that it was true.

Pulling open the top drawer, she picked out panties, socks and a sports bra, then paused, clutching them all in her hands. Turning to one side and then the other, she examined herself in the dresser's large mirror, looking at her body this way and that. She was in fantastic shape for her age, she had to admit it—slim, toned, a nice amount of muscle but the right amount of curves. She wouldn't go so far as to call herself perfect, but she was as close as could be. She worked hard to stay so in shape, and she knew that it showed.

"Doesn't make much difference, though, does it?" she mumbled absently, laying her palm flat against her stomach. When Michael did the same, he could reach practically from one side of her body to the other. He had enormous hands. "Doesn't keep your husband in bed with you, does it?"

After a moment's more appraisal, she pushed the drawer closed and went on with her dressing, gearing up in sweats and sneakers, her hair in a ponytail. After strapping her iPod to her arm, she went downstairs and left a note for Patrick on the refrigerator: "Went for a walk, be back to make breakfast. Love you!" A few stretches on the front porch and she took off down the road, destination unknown.

Though she walked regularly for exercise—or, often, just to relieve her everyday stress—she never had a planned-out route, preferring instead just to go where her feet wanted to take her. Today, she turned right out of the driveway and headed in the direction of the newly risen sun, enjoying that moment between twilight and full daybreak when the air seemed tinged with color and full of anticipation. Setting the iPod on one of her favorite playlists, she walked slowly for a while, warming up and letting the fresh air clear out her mind.

After half a mile, she felt sufficiently warmed up—and sufficiently over her self-pitying mood. Pushing up the sleeves of her sweatshirt, she picked up the pace and pushed her legs to carry her onward a little bit faster, enjoying the rush that came from really throwing herself into it.

What were you worried about? she thought, smiling. *You've got much more important things to think about.*

She turned up the volume on her iPod and, as the music swelled into her ears, her head swam with memories of the previous afternoon, images and sensations floating pleasantly through her mind: the soft sofa, the velvet pillows; the gold shag rug and the low light of the silk-shaded lamps. Reaching back into her mind, she recalled the feeling of the satin sheets on the bed, their slippery coolness, but barely dared to think about how warm Michael's skin had been as they'd wrapped around each other like puzzle pieces, or the weight of his body on top of hers. She certainly didn't want to linger on the way he'd looked into her eyes the whole time, as if he could see straight through to her very soul.

But that was indeed what she found herself doing— lingering and, honestly, enjoying every minute of it.

Yesterday changed everything, she thought, checking her pedometer. A mile gone, but time for a few more before she was due at home. Hanging a left, she decided to go down a road she'd traveled once or twice before, an out-of-the-way side street carved into a hillside, with a fantastic view of the city off in the distance.

Everything is different now, she told herself, trying to get used to the fact of it. Though she wasn't entirely sure where things with Michael would go from there, she knew that her time with him at the Chateau Deneuve had been more than something special; it had been intense, important, life altering. Before then, sure, she'd felt some attraction toward him, some inexplicable sense that something bigger than themselves had drawn them together. For what purpose, she hadn't known; toward what end, she'd had yet to see.

Now, she understood everything. They *were* soul mates; they were meant to be together. Whatever had brought them to the same place at the same time at last—

karma, a divine power, fate—she could no longer deny that it was simply meant to be.

But what about your family? a small voice in the back of her brain asked her, and she stopped short, nearly tripping on her own feet. Breathing heavily, she leaned over and put her hands on her thighs. All of a sudden, she felt a little nauseous.

"Oh, God, what about them?" she panted, wiping the sweat from her forehead with the back of her wrist. David was one thing; she'd long ago reconciled herself to the fact that they would never have a perfect marriage, that he would never be able to give her the sort of love and attention that she needed. If she hadn't met Michael, she was sure, something else would have torn them apart eventually. It really only was a matter of time.

But what about the children? she asked herself with that same voice of conscience. How would they have reacted if they knew what she was doing? Patrick might have gotten through it okay; he was practically an adult, and he had to know that his parents weren't entirely happy together. He might not have liked it, Carolina reasoned, but he would have accepted it one way or the other. The girls, on the other hand—well, she had no idea what she would ever tell them if it came down to it.

Having caught her breath, Carolina stood up straight and stepped over toward the edge of the road, where a steep drop-off led to an embankment below. At the edge of this miniature cliff, she could see the city in the distance and all the other hills and roadways that led up to it.

"I know you're out there somewhere," she said to the air, picturing Michael in her mind, his black helmet and orange-tinted sunglasses, coasting along some winding, hilly road on his bike. She knew he was out there just like she was, getting in his early morning exercise. And she wondered what he was thinking about while he did so, if she was at all on his mind.

Somehow, she knew that she was. And she also knew that whatever was going to happen, she just had to let it. This wasn't her choice anymore; this was her fate. If she was supposed to end up with Michael, she would, and all of the other details would fall into place—somehow, some time, some day.

Suddenly missing him terribly, she reached into her jacket pocket to pull out her cell phone—but found, to her dismay, that it wasn't there.

"Oh, no," she muttered, checking all her pockets in her jacket and her pants. She turned around in a circle, looking on the ground around her. Maybe it had fallen out somewhere…but no, she couldn't find it.

Jogging back up the street, she scanned the road, thinking that maybe it had bounced out of her pocket while she'd been walking, but after a short while, she had to stop and rethink the situation.

"I got up," she recalled, "got dressed, got my iPod, left a note for Patrick—"

Eyes wide, mouth hanging open in shock, Carolina realized what had happened to her cell phone. In her mind's eye, she pictured it exactly where she'd left it: sitting on the island in the kitchen, flipped open, ready to receive Michael's usual morning picture message.

"Oh, *no!*" she cried aloud, turning around and beginning to sprint back toward home. As she ran, she pictured her son coming downstairs for breakfast and finding the phone sitting there, Michael's grinning face staring out at him. What if he picked it up? What if he read the text messages Michael had been sending her—all the love notes and the details of the plans they'd made, all the things he'd said last night, after leaving the hotel with her…

"Carolina, what are you doing!" she yelled at herself, as she had so many times before. Panting as she struggled up a hill, she suddenly realized that her whole life had begun to revolve around that phone. How many hours had she spent writing text messages, or waiting for new ones to come in? It had gotten to the point where she couldn't function without Michael, couldn't get through the day—let alone an hour, or a minute—without hearing from him.

Seeing her house just a block away, she put all her energy into running until she burst through the back door, directly into the kitchen. The whole place was silent; the kids, she assumed, were still in bed. And there, on the island, was her cell phone, exactly as she pictured it.

Just as she reached out for it, it began to vibrate.

Receiving message, it said, and for a moment Carolina's hand froze in the air above it, waiting to see what would come in.

And then there was Michael's face, his hair damp, his eyes squinting in the sun. The familiar blue sky behind him, the mountain in the distance. He'd taken off his helmet and sunglasses this time, but the smile was still there—bigger, brighter and, somehow, more peaceful than ever.

Love you so much, he'd typed out underneath it. *With all my heart.*

"Me too," Carolina replied, snapping up the phone and putting it into her pocket before anyone came in and saw it.

Nineteen

Behind the wheel of Carolina's SUV, Michael rolled down the window and inhaled deeply, taking in the scent of the woods surrounding them.

"What is it?" Carolina asked from the passenger's seat, laughing a little.

He looked over at her and laughed, too. She sat so comfortably, turned a little toward him, one leg curled up underneath her—and both hands covering her eyes. A precaution, he had told her, to ensure that the surprise he'd arranged for her would not be prematurely revealed.

"Fresh air," he replied, not wanting to give away too much. "Gotta love it."

Taking one hand off her eyes and grabbing for the handle of the door next to her, Carolina let out a little yelp as the vehicle bounced along down a dirt road. Even though she couldn't see it, she could tell that it was unpaved and full of potholes. "Careful with my car, now," she teased Michael.

"Hey, don't look," he said, stretching over to put a hand across her eyes as well.

Reaching up again, Carolina laid her hand over his and gently ran her fingers along his knuckles. "I'm not looking," she told him softly, taking his hand and moving it down onto her cheek, leaning her face into his palm and slowly turning her head back and forth. She adored this feeling, the touch of her skin against his, so simple and yet so electric. "I swear."

"Good." Michael stepped hard on the gas for a moment, revving the engine to get the SUV up one last hill. Finally, he brought it to a stop, dust puffing up into the air around the tires.

In the ensuing stillness, Carolina smiled and raised her eyebrows. "Can I look now?" she asked eagerly.

Laughing, Michael unsnapped his seatbelt, leaned over and surprised her with a quick kiss. "Yes, you may, my love," he whispered to her, peeling her fingers away from her eyes and turning her head toward the passenger's side window.

Carolina gasped. "Oh, Michael." They were parked outside a small, secluded log cabin, its wraparound porch looking out over a clear, blue lake. Overhead, the sky was blue and the sun was shining; all around them, birds sang from their hiding spots in the oak and pine trees. Inhaling deeply, just as Michael had moments earlier, Carolina smiled wide.

"Oh, *Michael,*" she said, turning to face him. "It's *beautiful.*"

Smiling back at her, he ran a hand over her hair and pulled her closer, wrapping his arms around her. "Surprise," he whispered, then kissed her slowly, savoring the taste of her lips. Pulling away again, he looked deep into her eyes. "I hope you'll be comfortable here. We have the place for the whole weekend."

Gazing back at him, Carolina felt deliciously lost for a moment. "The whole weekend," she repeated, her mind wandering to all the things they could do together there, so far away from civilization, free of all the cares of their everyday lives. "I wish we could stay forever."

**

"Oh, good choice!" Carolina said as she took a bottle of wine out of one of the shopping bags Michael had unloaded from the car.

Across the open area of the cabin, crouching in front of the fireplace in the living room, a small broom and dustpan in his hands, he looked up at her. "You like red, right?"

"I *love* red," she said, setting the bottle on the counter and reaching into the bag to unpack the rest of the supplies. "Well," she said finally, standing in front of the open refrigerator, "I believe we're set for food through the next millennium."

Putting down the broom and dustpan, Michael stood up and brushed some stray soot off his jeans. "I know, I got too much," he said, laughing. "I just wanted to make sure that you're comfortable, that you don't have to think about anything this weekend except relaxing and enjoying yourself."

Leaning back against the counter, Carolina smirked at him. "Does that mean you're going to do all the cooking?"

Michael walked over to her slowly, smiling back at her, looking her up and down. He could tell that she was liking this surprise of his, that he had managed to pull it off. She was happy, he could tell; it showed in her face, her smile, her posture, her entire body. And for that, he was glad—and a little relieved. This weekend had taken so much planning, he hadn't been sure if he would be able to pull it all off. For Carolina, it had been easy enough; her husband, as usual, was out of town on a business trip. But Michael had had to tell Julie that he was going to a medical conference down in California. He wasn't a liar, never had been. That had been the toughest part of all of this.

Still, there he was. He'd done it. And now, seeing Carolina standing in front of him, her seductive smile, the way she looked at him, her eyes half closed, he knew that all the planning had been worth it.

"All the cooking," he agreed, coming up in front of her and grabbing her by the waist, then lifting her up easily to sit on the counter. As she put her arms around his shoulders, he closed his eyes and rested his cheek against hers, taking in the scent of her perfume, her skin, her hair. To him, it was better than the fresh mountain air outside the cabin. "Anything for you," he said, then brought his lips to meet hers once more.

In the silence of the cabin, Carolina moaned softly, feeling the rush of blood to her head that she always experienced whenever Michael touched her and especially when they kissed. There was more to it than simple passion; this wasn't just a physical affair they were having. This was something real, solid, tangible, but at the same time inexplicable, spiritual, on another level of reality. This was something that was truly meant to be, and it left her reeling.

"Michael," she said as their lips parted and he moved down to kissing her neck, so gently it sent shivers down her spine. Involuntarily, she brought a leg up to wrap around his waist; one arm still around his shoulder, her other hand ran through his hair, grabbing it as his teeth grazed the tender skin below her jaw, his warm breath coming out ragged and heavy.

"Michael," she repeated, gasping a bit as his hands came up and began unbuttoning her shirt. "Does this place have a bed?"

Standing up suddenly, Michael looked at her for a moment, the hint of a smile on his lips. Then, in one swift motion, he picked her up from the counter and carried her across the cabin, striding as quickly as he could toward the stairs to the loft.

***

"Mmm, that smells *good*," Carolina said, reaching to take the mug of coffee from Michael, then wrapping herself up in the warm fleece blanket once again. In front of her, the growing fire blazed in the hearth; it was still light outside, but the sun was low in the sky and Michael had decided to start the fire to stave off the evening chill. Bringing the blanket up more tightly around her bare shoulders, Carolina was thankful that he had.

Taking a seat beside her on the floor, wearing nothing but his jeans, Michael took a sip from his own cup, winking at her over the brim as he drank. "So," he said, setting the mug down on the slate tiles in front of the fireplace. "It's only Friday. We have two full days left. Do you think you can handle it?"

Carolina smiled at him, her cheeks flushing. They'd just spent the afternoon in bed, making love, talking, just staring into each other's eyes. It had been pure bliss, happiness like she hadn't known in more years than she cared to remember. Did she think she could stand more of the same for the rest of the weekend?

"Definitely," she said. "Nothing I'd rather do. Nowhere else I'd rather be."

Holding his hands out to feel the warmth of the fire, Michael looked at her. "And you really were surprised?"

Carolina nodded. "I was! I had no idea where you were taking me, even before you told me to cover my eyes. And I never would have guessed it would be here." She drank some more of her coffee and watched as Michael picked up an iron poker and rearranged the logs a little. "Have you been here before?" she asked him, curious about how he found the place.

He shrugged a little. "Not this cabin, no. I've been in the area, though. Mountain biking. A long time ago." Holding the poker still, he paused for a moment, staring into the fire as if remembering that trip. Carolina noted that he didn't look too happy.

"Had a bad time?" she asked gently, reaching out from under her blanket to put a hand on his bare back.

Still leaning forward to reach the fire, he turned his head to look back at her. "No, no," he said quickly, smiling though it seemed a little forced. "I was just thinking..." He lay the poker down on the slate, then shimmied himself back to sit beside Carolina. She opened her blanket with her arm, and he nestled inside with her.

"Thinking what?" she asked gently, resting her head on his shoulder and closing her eyes. This posture was so comfortable, came so naturally to her.

"That it's been a long time since I've been able to do anything like that. I went away for the weekend with a few friends. We just took our bikes and roamed the hills all day, then stayed at a cabin like this at night... Barbecued some meat, drank some beer, just had a good time... I don't get to do things like that much anymore."

Sighing, Carolina knew exactly how he felt. "I don't even remember the last time I went away anywhere, with friends or anyone else."

For a few minutes, they just sat there, wrapped in the blanket and listening to the fire crackle in front of them. Outside, the sun cast its bright-orange glow across the surface of the lake and the birds put away their melodies for the night. A slight wind blew, rustling the leaves of the trees above the roof.

"Michael," Carolina began, her voice tentative, but Michael cut her off.

"You're not going to say 'what are we doing here' again, are you?" he asked her with a bit of a laugh.

Carolina raised her head and looked at him. He returned her gaze, disturbed by how cloudy her eyes appeared, by the trouble that seemed knitted into her brow.

"I was just joking," he said to her, bringing a hand up to her face, running the backs of his fingers across her cheek. He settled his palm on her neck and looked at her imploringly. "You know I was joking, right?"

Carolina smiled at him, but it was a wan expression. "I know," she said, "but, well, we do have to talk about it, don't we? I mean, we can't just keep pretending that we're two young people in love, without a care in the world. We have cares. We have families. We both have a lot to lose by pursuing this relationship."

Michael sighed and closed his eyes, bowed his head. Thinking, he reached for his coffee cup again and took a drink, then looked back at Carolina. "You're right," he said. "We do. But I think it's worth it. Whatever I have to do to be with you is worth it."

Carolina drank, too, looking into the fire as she thought. "But don't you feel bad about it?" She looked back at Michael, her eyes imploring him to give her an answer that would quiet her mind. "Don't you feel...*guilty?*"

Setting his cup down again, Michael turned to face her more fully, reaching into the blanket to grab one of her hands in both of his. He looked down at their hands for a moment, running his fingers lightly over her palm, her wrist, her forearm. "More than I can express," he said, his voice low. "I'm not a monster, you know. I am a committed husband and a devoted father." He looked up at Carolina, the seriousness of his gaze now surprising her. "But I also love you. With all of my heart—with *more than* all of my heart. With everything that I have, everything that I am. Carolina, I can't explain it but from the moment I met you, I knew that we were meant to be together. I feel like—"

"Like we've known each other all our lives?" she finished for him, their eyes locking in that hypnotic way they did when both she and Michael were thinking the same thing. "Or maybe longer?"

Staring into her eyes raptly, Michael nodded. "Like I've loved you for a hundred years. Like we've gone through all of this before." He put a hand up to his heart, his other hand still gripping hers tightly. "Carolina, I love my family, but in front of you, everything else in my life just falls away. Whatever's happening here with us, we just have to let it happen. There's no stopping it now. Do you know what I mean? Do you understand how I feel?"

"Michael," Carolina said, feeling the pressure of tears behind her eyes. Putting her coffee cup aside, she leaned forward and let her blanket drop to the floor, then propelled herself into his arms, the only place she ever really wanted to be. "I do," she said, covering his face with kisses. "I do, I do."

TWENTY

For days after their weekend at the lake house, Michael simply couldn't think of anything but Carolina. When he went to bed at night, he closed his eyes and saw her face, that way she smiled just for him. In his dreams, they were together, just the two of them alone, and everything was perfect. As soon as he awoke each morning, he jumped right out of bed to go and send her an email or a text message.

It's just us, he wrote one day. *No one else and nothing else matters. Only you and me, together forever.*

The next day he told her, *You make me feel alive. No one has ever had this effect on me.*

The next, *You are so beautiful inside and out, Carolina. You are flawless. I'm so lucky to have found you.*

First thing every day, he had some thought for her, some words about how much he loved her, desired her, wanted to be with her forever. He told her about specific memories he had—a certain way she'd touched him or looked at him, the way the sun had glanced off her hair one afternoon, a conversation they'd had. He told her about his fantasies of taking her away from it all somehow, of running away with her and leaving everything else behind. He shared with her every notion that came to him, every emotion that he felt in his heart.

You and your daydreams, she wrote to him one day after he'd sent her an email about buying a boat and taking her on a year-long cruise—another random idea that had just come to him. He could picture her laughing, her bright, beautiful smile, as she sent it.

But it wasn't a daydream, not in Michael's mind. Though he didn't know how—or if—he could ever make it happen, being alone with Carolina had become an all-encompassing thought to him: running away, starting a new life, building a home and just finally being able to be together, as they were fated to be. He thought about it constantly—when he rode his bike, when he drove to work, when he talked to his patients. No matter what he did, Carolina was always on his mind. He was always thinking about how he had to be with her no matter what.

"But wouldn't it be great?" he asked her one afternoon, spinning around on his creaky, old chair and propping a foot up on the windowsill behind his desk. Outside, summer was waning; the sun was shining but not as blisteringly as it had been for so many months. Michael's mind wandered back to all the days he had spent out there with Carolina, at the Chateau Deneuve, at the cabin by the lake, at out-of-the-way restaurants and walking around the city's parks, hiding under the boughs of the trees to kiss, to hold on to one another tightly. They were just small pieces of time, stolen moments here and there, much too few and far between. "If we could be together all the time?"

On the other end of the call, Carolina sighed. Though Michael had never been in her office, he could picture her sitting behind a desk, gazing out a window just as he was, her green eyes twinkling in the sunlight reflected off the city's skyscrapers. "Of course it would be great," she said, sounding a little forlorn. "I want to be with you all the time, Michael. I feel lost when I'm without you, like we're linked

together. Like I can't survive without you." She sighed
again. "But running away…that's not reality. Right now—"

"Right now I love you," he interrupted, unable to hold
himself back, unwilling to hear her reasons why they
shouldn't have accepted their fate. "And I want to be with
you no matter what. Carolina, I don't care about reality. *You
are my reality now.*"

He paused for a moment, watched one of his patients
strolling up the walkway to the building. He checked his
watch—almost time for his three-fifteen appointment. "And
if the reality is that we can only see each other every few
days, and have to stay hidden away from the world…" He
sighed as well and turned back to his desk. He glanced at the
framed picture of his wife and kids; they looked back at him
expectantly. "Well, then, I guess I'll have to accept that…*for
now.* But you can't expect me to live without you in my arms
forever."

Carolina laughed a little. Michael pictured her again,
saw her tossing her hair back from her shoulder, putting her
thumb up to her mouth to bite her nail a little, something she
did sometimes when she was coming up with one of her
brilliant ideas. He saw the corners of her red-painted lips
curling up into a grin, and he couldn't help doing the same
himself.

"Can you get away today?" Carolina asked him, her
voice low. "Meet me at the chateau?"

"Well…" Michael reached over and turned the picture
of his family away a little, at least so their eyes weren't
boring into him. Then he looked at his watch again. "One
last appointment today," he told Carolina, and then paused.
He pictured her again, her long legs, her high heels. He
wondered what she was wearing, and what she was wearing
underneath it. "But to be with you," he added, "I think I can
cancel it."

***

Whistling a light tune as he walked out of his office, Michael put on his jacket and slipped his cell phone into his pocket. Walking down the hallway toward the reception area, he glanced inside an exam room and saw his partner with a patient. Michael quickened his pace before Scott could see him.

"Marissa," he said, pausing at the front desk where his assistant sat. "I need to cancel my three-fifteen."

The young woman peered out over the high top of her desk, at a man sitting in the waiting room—the same man Michael had seen out his window.

"Dr. Sanford," Marissa said, leaning over toward him and whispering. "He's already here."

"Oh, yeah," Michael said, letting out a breath, puffing out his cheeks as he thought. "Well, just tell him—"

In his pocket, his cell phone buzzed, and he reached in and quickly whipped it out. Flipping it open, he found a text message from Carolina.

Do you believe that things happen for a reason? it asked. He stared down at the phone, considering the question.

"Dr. Sanford?" Marissa asked. He did not respond. "Dr. Sanford?"

Still gazing at his opened cell phone, Michael wondered what Carolina had on her mind. Did he think that things happened for a reason? He guessed that he did—at least, he had since he'd met Carolina. Before then, he'd simply stumbled through his life without much of a higher purpose, letting things happen to him instead of actively going after what he'd wanted—without, now that he thought about it, really even knowing *what* he'd wanted. He'd married Julie because they'd been dating for a while and it was time;

they'd had children because that was what married couples did. He'd worked in a hospital because he'd interned there and they'd offered him the position when he'd graduated. When he'd gotten tired of that, he'd joined a practice with the first colleague who had asked him.

For the first time now, he was ready to take charge of his life, to go after what he wanted—and get it. Carolina inspired that sort of passion in him.

"*Dr. Sanford,*" Marissa whispered loudly through clenched teeth, finally drawing his attention. "What should I tell your three-fifteen?"

"Oh, uh, tell him I was called out on an emergency," he said, beginning to type something into his phone. "I'll go out the back door."

"You're going to sneak out?" his assistant asked. "For real?"

He paused his typing and looked at her, a little surprised that she would talk to him like that.

"Dr. Sanford," she went on, "I know that what you do or how you handle your patients isn't my business, but I really feel like I have to say something here because now this involves me. You're asking me to go out there and lie to this guy who already took time out of his day to show up here, and for what? Why are you leaving in the middle of the day again?"

"Again?" Michael asked with a bit of a nervous laugh. "When do I leave in the middle of the day?"

"At least once a week," Marissa told him. "Maybe you think I don't notice, but I do. I also see you holing up in your office and spending all your time between appointments on the phone. You're two weeks behind on your paperwork, and you're not even scheduling as many patients as you used to. Over the last three months, your appointments have gone down by about a third. Dr. Sanford, this just isn't like you."

Michael just looked at her for a moment. Had he really been pulling away from his work so much? He hadn't noticed; it sure hadn't felt like it. He'd been so focused on Carolina, nothing else had seemed to matter.

Carolina, he thought, checking his watch. He had told her he'd meet up with her in fifteen minutes. He had to get out of there.

"Listen, Marissa," he said, "I've been busy. I've had some things going on. Just help me out now and I'll get back on top of things as soon as I can, alright?"

Still seated behind her desk, Marissa folded her arms and looked at him skeptically.

"I'll owe you one, okay?" Michael said, then walked away from the desk, down the hall and toward the rear exit.

Once outside, he paused and took a deep breath of the humid afternoon air, running a hand through his hair as he did so. It felt good to be free, but that exchange with Marissa had him worried. He hadn't realized that he was being so obvious, that anyone had noticed that his attention had been somewhere other than his work. It was clear to him now that he couldn't call Carolina from work anymore. He would have to find some other way to keep in touch with her.

He looked down at his cell phone again, still clutched in his hand.

Do you believe that things happen for a reason?

Everything happens for a reason, he'd started to type back in the office, while Marissa had been ranting at him. Smiling now, he finished his message. *You and I happened. That's the only proof that I need.*

TWENTY-ONE

Michael had been into cycling for quite some time. He wouldn't say he was a professional, but an avid cyclist he was. This was definitely a sport he had always enjoyed, and through years of practice, he had become good at it. He had invested a lot of money in his road bike as well as all the best gear—a good helmet (his number-one priority), padded shorts, shoes with clips so his feet never left the pedals during his ride. He also had a computerized odometer to track how many miles he rode. On a good ride, he did about forty miles. On a great ride, he might have reached a hundred.

This Tuesday, the first day of September, was going to be just a so-so day. The sun was only half out; the sky was murky gray in color. It had rained overnight and the roads were slick, some areas coated with a combination of water and oil. The temperature was on the cooler side. Michael had to go back into the house before he left to get a warmer, long-sleeved cycling jersey.

From that point on, it had pretty much been downhill—metaphorically, at least. By the time he was struggling up the third enormous incline on his regular route, sweating and grunting as he pushed his feet into the pedals, he was wishing that he'd picked another of his usual courses, one where he could have coasted a little more. The weather, the temperature and all the thoughts in his mind were just coming together in a perfect storm, making his normally enjoyable ride just another difficult task he had to complete.

Stopping at the crest of the hill, he unclipped his shoes from the pedals and stood at the side of the road, straddling his bike as he took off his helmet. In his earphones, one song ended and another began, an odd, out-of-place love song. He took his iPod off the band that secured it to his arm and looked at it, wondering how this tune had made it into his normal riding mix.

Everything happens for a reason, he reminded himself, smiling a little as he put the iPod back in place.

Deciding to rest for a minute and catch his breath, Michael leaned back on the bike seat again and just listened to the music, letting it take him back to the only place his mind ever wanted to go anymore: to Carolina, to her smile, to the sound of her voice. Closing his eyes, he took a deep breath and thought about their time at the hotel the previous afternoon. Whenever they were together, it was magical, amazing, so perfect… It was so clear to the both of them at this point that they were meant to be together, that fate had brought them into one another's lives. There was more to their relationship than just physical attraction. When he looked into Carolina's eyes, he knew that they were connected on a deeper level, that they were bonded together, somehow, by time and space itself.

And then, with a sigh, his mind involuntarily began to replay the scene that had unfolded when he'd gone home the previous evening. Once again, in living color, he saw the reproving look Julie had given him as soon as he'd walked into the house, the impatient, annoyed sound of her voice when she'd demanded to know where he'd been. She'd been trying to call him, she'd said, to ask him to pick the kids up from school because she'd had some errands to do. He'd bowed his head and listened to her tirade, then simply said that he'd been tied up all day with patients, though Julie hadn't seemed to care much at all what his answer was. She'd seemed much more interested in lecturing him about how precious her own time was, and how pretty much everything he ever did was wrong.

Closing his eyes, Michael hung his head again now, remembering how this discussion with his wife had turned into an all-out fight. The memory of it just left him feeling completely defeated all over again. Though he usually tried to calm his wife, last night, he'd just been under too much stress already, and he'd given in. He'd argued with her. They'd raised their voices; they'd both said things they shouldn't have. The children had gone and hidden in their bedrooms. When Michael had gone to apologize to them later and assure them that everything was alright, Emily had seemed so sad, and Josh had barely even looked at him. They were just as tired of the tension in their home as he was. He could tell.

"So, what are you going to do about it?" he asked himself aloud, raising his head once more and looking down the road ahead, the steep, twisting downhill that awaited him. He thought for a moment, but no answers came to him. He shrugged. "Well, at least you're going to finish your ride. Maybe that will help."

After putting his helmet back on, he slowly pushed his bike with one foot toward the road's point of decline. Pausing just a moment at the edge, he stared down the hill, focusing on the turn at bottom, picturing the winding road that lay beyond it. He'd ridden this route a hundred times; he knew it by heart. It was fast, a real challenge. Just what he needed, he thought, to clear his mind.

Clipping his shoe onto the pedal, he set off, coasting down the first leg of the hill into a tuck position. Focusing on that turn at the bottom, he felt the wind brushing against his cheeks, the humidity of the air as he breathed it in. The pulse of the song still playing in his ears. Carolina's name reverberating through his mind.

At the turn, he leaned down low over the handlebars, making his body more aerodynamic, and steered into the curve, whipping around it at breakneck speed. A short straightaway followed, and he pedaled as hard as he could, trying to outrun the thoughts that were threatening to overtake him.

Carolina, he thought with every push of his feet. *Carolina, Carolina, Carolina.*

A hard left and he was angling around the next turn already—a long one, more flat, less downhill. He continued pedaling, working hard to maintain the pace he'd already set.

What are you going to do about it? he asked himself again, knowing that he had to come up with an answer. He couldn't go on like this, couldn't continue living a life that he knew was—

"It's a lie!" he shouted suddenly into the wind that rushed across his face, sending a chill down his back, his feet working furiously. Another turn came up, another left, and he was downhill again—but this time pedaling to propel himself even faster, as fast as the thoughts that raced through his head. His marriage. His career. His entire life. All of it meant nothing. All of it was false in the face of what he had with Carolina. A sham. Something that had gotten him by, helped him pass the time until the moment when she had walked into his life.

"A lie!" he said again, the truth of the word hitting him full force. Though he loved his wife—and his children; he loved them more than anything—he saw his relationship with Julie now for what it was. They hadn't been in love in years; perhaps they never had been. He'd just been a compliant husband for her to push around, to treat like another child. She had never seen him as an equal, and he had put her on a higher pedestal than she had deserved.

But it's not her fault, he thought now, tears springing to his eyes. Making his way down another straight segment of the road, he slowed down a bit and let go of the handlebars. Sitting up straight on the bike, he rubbed his eyes with his fingers as he kept on pedaling. He squinted them shut tightly for a moment, trying to clear them, then opened them and focused once again on the road ahead of him—and on what he knew he had to do.

"But it's not my fault, either," he said, leaning over onto the handlebars once again as another steep downgrade loomed in front of him. He pedaled furiously, propelling himself toward the hill as hard as he could.

Carolina, Carolina, Carolina, he thought in time with the movement of his feet, the music in his ears. *We must be together. Now and forever. I'll give up everything for you. Everything, everything, everything.*

Nearing the bottom of the hill and another deeply banked curve, a peace began to wash over him, and he smiled wide for the first time all morning. Suddenly, it seemed, a weight had been lifted from his shoulders. He realized what he had to do; he made his decision. He chose to be with Carolina no matter what sacrifices he had to make, no matter what the consequences. She was worth it; *they* were worth it. This was the only option that made sense to him, and he had to follow through on it.

"Yes!" he cried out, feet pedaling faster, his excitement building. He had never felt so sure of anything in his life, and he couldn't contain it. "Yes!" he shouted again, feeling like his voice, his joy, could reach the tops of the mountains that he saw off in the distance. He looked out at them for a moment, taking his eyes off the quickly approaching turn.

And then in an instant, he was flying through the air, and his shouts were no longer full of elation but laced with terror.

Landing hard against the trunk of an enormous tree nestled in the neck of the road's bend, Michael cried out in pain, an electric jolt radiating from his head straight down his spine and into his legs. Twenty feet away, his bike lay against the guardrail separating the roadway from the grassy hill beyond it, a mangled mess—bent rims, a flat tire, chain falling off.

"Oh, God," he moaned, reaching up to unclip his helmet and pull it off his head.

Looking back up the road, Michael found the source of this accident: another slick spot left over from last night's storm, a puddle of rainwater mixed with oil, more than likely from a leaky truck engine. A recipe for disaster for anyone coming down that hill headfirst in excess of thirty miles an hour.

"And not looking at what they're doing," he muttered, cursing himself for ever taking his eyes off the road. He'd been reckless, foolish. He never should have let his happiness overrule his own safety.

But then, he remembered what he'd been happy about. "Carolina," he said softly, laying his head back against the ground and looking up into the tops of the trees surrounding him, to the sky beyond. A tuft of clouds was just parting right overhead, letting a few random sunbeams through. They shone directly down upon his face, so brightly that he had to close his eyes.

Everything is okay, he told himself, trying to ignore the lingering pain in his back, the bruises and scrapes he could feel on his arms and legs. *Everything is good. I'm going to be with Carolina forever.* He opened his eyes, blinking back tears in the dazzling sunlight. *How can anything be wrong ever again?*

Bringing a hand up to shield his eyes, with the other hand he reached into the pocket of his sweatshirt and withdrew his cell phone. Thankfully, it had survived the crash and still seemed to be in working order. Flipping it open, he brought up a new text message and typed out a message to Carolina as fast as he could with his aching hands. He didn't tell her about what had happened here; he knew that she would be getting her kids ready for school and didn't want her to worry. He didn't even tell her about the decision he'd made. Somehow, he just knew that she would already know.

Run away with me. That was all that it said. And he sent it out to her, knowing that it would be enough.

TWENTY-TWO

"Michael Sanford!" Carolina shouted over the top of the desk at the nurses' station. In the middle of the emergency room, the area was bustling with medical personnel and crowded with carts full of medications, surgical supplies and half-empty food trays. Across the desk, phones rang and patient records sat open, waiting to be looked at. And in the middle of it all sat one woman sifting through a stack of prescriptions.

"Michael Sanford?" Carolina said to her again, trying to gain her attention through the noise and distractions. Slowly, and with a look of supreme annoyance on her face, the woman raised her head a little and adjusted her glasses, then trained her tired-looking eyes on Carolina's face.

"May I help you?" the woman asked, her voice just as slow as her movements.

"Yes," Carolina replied, trying not to sound too hysterical or overly rude. She realized that this woman probably had a difficult job, and that dealing with the public—especially people in emergency situations—was probably pretty tiring. "I'm looking for a patient by the name of Michael Sanford. I received a call that he was taken here after an accident of some sort."

In slow motion, the woman put down her pile of prescriptions and pushed herself on her wheeled chair to a file cart full of hanging folders that stood near the wall behind the desk. She pawed the tabs of the folders for a minute, then looked languidly back at Carolina. "What did you say the last name was again?"

"Sanford!" Carolina practically shouted, leaning over the desk as if getting closer to this woman would somehow make her speed up.

After flipping through the folders for another minute, the woman retrieved what Carolina assumed to be Michael's file. Wheeling herself back over to the desk, the woman opened the folder and perused it over the tops of her glasses. "Michael Sanford," she muttered to herself, licking her finger and using it to turn the first page. "He was brought in with possible head trauma, is that correct?"

"Head trauma!" Carolina repeated. She hadn't heard any such thing.

About an hour earlier, just after watching Patrick pull out of the driveway and head off to school, the girls in the backseat of the car, she'd gone back into the house and found her cell phone ringing, and Michael's number on the caller ID.

That's strange, she had thought, hesitating for a moment before answering it, wondering why he would be calling her so early in the day. He sent her text messages every morning, and the usual pictures during his daily bike ride, but he never, ever called her until they were both at their offices—and recently, there'd been even less of that. Something about his secretary being suspicious; he hadn't really explained it to Carolina very well. In fact, he'd seemed very disturbed by the whole thing. He'd just said that they had to stick mostly to their text messages and emails for the time being.

And that had been just fine with Carolina. She loved reading what he wrote to her; his words were so full of emotion, so insightful. Each message was a love letter, a profession of his devotion to her, a declaration of the beauty of their relationship. It was like he listened to whatever his heart was telling him and wrote it down, then sent it off to her, to ensure that she would know exactly how he was feeling. The funny thing was, she already knew.

"Hello?" she had said as she'd answered the call on her cell phone that morning.

"Uh, yes, this is a paramedic from Harborview Medical Center," a voice had replied—a voice that was decidedly not Michael's. "I'm calling for a…a Carolina? Is that you, ma'am?"

"Yes," Carolina had said, her tone a bit suspicious. Why was this person calling from Michael's phone? And from a hospital, no less? "What's going on? Is Michael okay?"

"Well, ma'am, he's been in a cycling accident and he called nine one one to ask for an ambulance."

"Oh, my God!" Carolina had exclaimed, reaching a hand out to steady herself against the kitchen counter. In a flash, her entire history with Michael flashed before her eyes: their meeting at the charity dinner, their first date, the Chateau Deneuve, the cabin by the lake. The hours they had spent on the phone, the times she'd stolen away from work just to see him. The hopes she had—small hopes, tiny hopes that she was even afraid to fully admit to herself, but hopes nonetheless—of just what the future might hold for them. "Is he alright? Can I talk to him?"

"Ma'am, I'm sorry but we had to sedate him so that he wouldn't move around, as we're unsure of what sort of injuries he's sustained as of this moment," the paramedic had informed her. "I'm in the ambulance with him right now and we're almost at the hospital. I just saw that he had his cell phone in his hand and yours was the last number he accessed. You're his wife, right?"

Trying hard to choke back the tears that welled in her eyes, Carolina didn't know what to say.

"Ma'am, can you meet us at the ER?"

Thankful that he had gone on without letting her explain just who she was, she had nodded her head, wiping the tears away from her flushed cheeks. "I'll be right there," she'd said, then grabbed her keys and headed out the door.

***

"He's in area four, dear, behind the last curtain on the left just down this hall."

Snapping back to the present, Carolina looked at the woman behind the desk for a moment.

"Curtain four, darlin'," the woman told her again, now even daring to look impatient.

"Okay, thanks," Carolina replied absently, then turned and headed off in the direction the woman had indicated.

You're his wife, right? The paramedic's words rang in Carolina's ears as she made her way down the hall, trying hard not to see all the pain and suffering going on around her. On one side was a child with his leg in a splint; on the other was an elderly woman with tubes in her arms and nose. Carolina put a hand up to her own forehead and once again attempted to stave off a crying jag. She was just so scared of what condition she would find Michael in—and terrified that she wouldn't be able to do a thing about it.

No, I'm not his wife, she thought. *I have no legal right to him. But I have his heart, and he has mine, and doesn't that count for something?*

Finally, she stood outside area number four. The light-blue curtain was closed, beyond it only silence and stillness. Pausing for a moment, Carolina wiped at her eyes one last time, reminding herself that she had to be brave, not for herself but for Michael. Whatever state he was in, no matter how badly he was injured, she had to be strong and just give him all the love that she could.

Holding her breath and closing her eyes, she reached a shaky hand up and grasped the edge of the curtain, then pulled it back slowly, scraping it noisily along its metal track on the ceiling. She steeled herself for whatever gruesome scene she would reveal, for the blood and the bandages and Michael's strong body now lying broken beyond repair.

"Hey!" He called to her from within the curtained area, sounding surprised—and, of course, thrilled—to see her there.

Carolina opened her eyes. "Michael," she replied, her voice cracking, something halfway between a laugh and a sob stuck in her throat. She just stood there for a moment, looking at him. The back of his bed upright, he sat erect, propped up on a few small, thin pillows. He wore a hospital gown, off-white with a green-diamond pattern on it, and had a white blanket over his legs. In his left wrist, an IV needle had been inserted, its tube leading to a bag of saline on a hanger by the bed. A strip of pristine, white gauze had been wrapped around his right forearm.

"Come in, come in!" he told her, his smile wider than she had ever seen it. He waved a hand, beckoning her to his bedside. "And close the curtain," he added quietly, now holding out both arms to her.

Quickly stepping into the exam area, Carolina did as he'd said and drew the curtain closed behind her, then made her way over to the side of the bed. Careful as she ever was whenever they were in public together, she did not get too close, didn't even touch him. Being so near to him without reaching out a hand to stroke his face, smooth his hair, run a finger along his lips, was torturous to her. She clasped her own hands together just to stop herself from trying.

But then, before she even knew what was happening, Michael had reached out for her, his free arm slipping inside her jacket and around her waist, pulling her body in close to his. He reeled her in until she leaned across the bed halfway on top of him, and held her there firmly as he kissed her.

"Michael," she said again as they broke apart, finally putting her hand up to his head and running her fingers through his hair. "Your head…"

"My head is fine," he told her quietly, kissing her quickly again. "I have a good helmet, remember?"

With a sigh of relief, Carolina did remember—and didn't know why she hadn't thought of it before. He'd bought a new helmet only a couple of weeks earlier; he'd told her all about it at the time.

"Top of the line," he'd told her. "Best money can buy. Nothing's more important than protecting your head."

"The woman at the front desk said you had a head injury," Carolina explained to him now, shifting her weight a little so she could sit next to him on the edge of the bed. "And the paramedic who called me said that you were sedated."

Michael laughed a little. "Oh, yeah, I guess I was trying to get up and walk or something, and they were afraid I was going to hurt myself more than I already was, so they gave me a shot to settle me down for the ride here." He paused and looked at her, into her eyes. "God, in that moment when I landed on the ground, I thought that I might never get to see those eyes again." He smiled at her. "You're the only thing I thought about. You're the one who got me through this."

This time, Carolina leaned in and kissed him, long and hard, her heart swelling with love and happiness. Only moments earlier, she'd been imagining how she could have gone on with her life if she'd lost him; now, she was only thankful that his injuries weren't serious. The whole experience had shaken her, but it had also made her see so much more clearly exactly how much she needed Michael in her life.

"I never want to lose you," she whispered to him, putting her arms around him as best she could and holding him close. "We can never be apart."

"And we won't be," Michael replied, pulling away from her a bit to look at her once again. Putting a hand on her cheek, he gazed at her deeply, becoming lost in her eyes. "We may be apart physically, but never in our minds or our hearts. We're meant to be together for eternity."

Putting a hand up to his face as well, Carolina rested her forehead against his. Outside their curtain, the hospital clamored; patients cried, doctors lectured, TVs blared and intercoms buzzed. But in their little room, separated from the world outside only by a flimsy piece of material, everything was silent, and perfect, and calm. They were together, Carolina thought, and everything was exactly as it was supposed to be.

***

"Did you get my text message?" Michael asked Carolina. For some time, she'd been fidgeting with his blanket, straightening it out, pulling it over his feet, folding the top down neatly at his waist. *Keeping herself busy,* he'd thought. *Convincing herself that there's really nothing wrong with me.*

Looking at him, Carolina lowered her eyebrows. She looked puzzled. "No," she said. "When did you send it?"

Michael laughed a little. "Right after my bike and I parted ways. Just before I called for the ambulance."

"Hm," Carolina replied, reaching for her purse on a nearby chair. Rifling through it, she found her cell phone and pulled it out. "Well, would you look at that," she said, holding it up for Michael to see. On the screen, a picture of an envelope flashed, indicating that she had an unread message. "I didn't even see it, what with the paramedic calling me and all." She looked at the phone for a moment, then at Michael. "Should I read it now?"

In the bed, Michael stretched out a bit, going to put his hands behind his head—and then remembering that he was still hooked up to the IV. Feeling the tug of the tube, he put his hands back on his lap and folded them, then smiled at Carolina and gave her a shrug. "It's up to you," he said, a bit of a devilish twinkle in his eye.

Noticing his look, Carolina smiled as well, then flipped open her phone and clicked into her messages. Opening the one unread one, she looked at it for only a moment, taking in the four small words displayed there. *Run away with me.* Then she looked back up at Michael. She didn't know what to say.

"Well, are you going to give me an answer?" he asked playfully, watching her for a response. He smiled still, but now he looked a little nervous, Carolina noticed, as if something really big was riding on her answer.

"Are you... Is this for real?" she asked him, not sure just what she should make of it. How many times had he asked her to go away with him, to get away from it all, to run off to the mountains or some secluded island or the south of France and never go home again? He had these daydreams, as she called them, practically on a daily basis, and he'd always described them to her. He had a thousand different scenarios that they enacted in his head, a thousand different ways for them to live happily ever after.

But something in his eyes told her that this time…this was no fantasy.

His face now serious, Michael reached out a hand to Carolina, and slowly she slipped her fingers into his. She just stood there for a moment, feeling the electricity running through this connection of their bodies, butterflies dancing around in the pit of her stomach.

"Michael," she whispered, looking down at their hands. "Are you really serious about this?"

She looked into his eyes then, and she saw there everything she needed to know. As she opened her mouth to give him her answer, however, the intercom—the portal to the hospital-wide paging system—on the wall behind the bed began to crackle.

"Dr. Novak," a voice said through it, monotone and scratchy, "please come to the nurses' desk to speak to the Sanford family."

Michael closed his eyes, his jaw set. "Julie," he said.

Carolina's eyes opened wide. "I have to go!" she said, grabbing her purse, pulling her hand away from Michael's—but he held on.

"What's your answer?" he asked her, his voice low and urgent, almost pleading.

Carolina paused, looking toward the opening in the curtain. Any moment, she feared, Michael's wife, perhaps with his children, would be coming down the hallway. She had to get out of there; she couldn't be seen with him. Not yet, not now, not like this.

"Carolina!" he said, squeezing her fingers.

"Yes," she told him quickly, looking back to him. "Yes," she repeated, and his face softened; his grip on her hand relaxed. He raised it to his lips and kissed the backs of her fingers, pressed them softly against his cheek.

"I love you," he said, his eyes closed. "I love you, Carolina."

"I love you too," she said, coming back to give him a fast kiss on the top of his head. And then she drew her hand out of his, and slipped away through the curtain.

Twenty-Three

At a table in the corner of a coffee shop, Michael cupped his hands around a warm mug of coffee, then lifted it to take a sip. He glanced at the doorway for what seemed like the hundredth time in the last five minutes, anxious for Carolina to arrive.

They'd met here before—a café on the edge of downtown, a place that was just busy enough that they wouldn't be noticed, not so trendy that they risked seeing anyone either of them knew. They'd sat at this same table before, facing the same window, their backs to the door, and sharing some drinks and some conversation. He remembered the first time, only a couple of weeks after they'd met. He remembered the last time, many months later, when they'd ended up at their favorite hotel afterwards.

"Sorry I'm late," Carolina said at last, coming up behind him and placing a hand on his shoulder. She set a cup down on the table and then shrugged off her coat and laid it across the spare chair on the other side of the table. Though Michael had loved the lighter, more revealing clothes she'd worn throughout the spring and summer, he had to admit that she looked devastating in a simple sweater and jeans. Carolina was so beautiful, he thought, she would have looked good to him in just about anything.

"It's only a few minutes," he told her, watching as she settled herself into a chair next to his. "Besides, I would wait for you all day if I had to."

Smiling, Carolina leaned over and gave him a quick kiss, though as she pulled away her eyes roamed the coffee shop.

"No one's here," he told her, trying not to sound too impatient. He hated all this sneaking around, the way they had to keep their love hidden—but understood as well why it made her so nervous to be seen with him. They both had so much to lose.

But if we're both giving it all up anyway... he thought, feeling a sudden surge throughout his body. He closed his eyes for a moment, remembering that moment in the hospital, two weeks before then, when she'd said yes to him. Yes, she would run away with him. Yes, she would leave everything behind.

"How's your arm feeling?" Carolina asked, drawing him back to the present.

"Ah, my arm," he said, pushing the sleeve of his shirt up a little to reveal the large Band-aid that had replaced the gauze bandage. "It's doing well. I took out the stitches this morning. I think it might scar, but it will be minimal."

"Oh," Carolina said sympathetically, putting a hand gently over his wound. "Does it hurt much?"

"Not at all," Michael told her, laying his hand over hers. "In fact, now that you're here, I don't even notice it at all."

For a moment, they simply looked at one another, a silent communication passing between them. This was no regular afternoon coffee date for them, no run-of-the-mill sneaking away from their responsibilities. They would not end up at the Chateau Deneuve; they would not simply drink their coffee and go home like nothing had happened.

No, they had agreed to meet there for a reason on this day, and when they were through with it, they both knew, their lives would never be the same.

"So, where do we start?" Carolina asked him as if she were running a meeting, raising her coffee cup to take a drink.

Michael sat back in his comfortable, overstuffed easy chair and looked out the window. Outside, it was rainy, a typical mid-fall day in Seattle. People ran down the sidewalks, from one doorway to another, huddled under their umbrellas, trying to dodge the raindrops. Everyone had somewhere to be...

Just like Carolina and I do, he thought, a smile beginning to grow from the thought of it.

"Well," he began, propping a foot up on the nearby windowsill. "We have to decide where to go."

Letting out a long, slow breath, Carolina sat back in her chair as well. She crossed her legs and held her mug in her hands, using its warmth to heat her chilly fingers. "How about somewhere warm?" she asked with a grin, looking at Michael, her eyebrows raised suggestively.

Still looking out the window, Michael nodded his head slowly, rubbing his chin in thought. "Warm sounds good," he agreed. "You mean like...Florida?"

At that suggestion, Carolina wrinkled up her nose and shook her head. "Been there, done that," she said. "Don't like it very much. Too humid, too many people."

"Okay," Michael said, taking the rejection in stride. He hadn't expected to hit this nail on the head in one try. "Somewhere more north? Atlanta? Virginia?"

"Virginia?" Carolina asked with a laugh. "Why Virginia?"

Michael looked at her, a little surprised by her amusement. "I have relatives there. It's a nice state." He laughed a little, too, though, realizing that perhaps it wasn't the most exotic destination. "Well, the moon is really nice there, anyway, when it's big and full."

At that, Carolina didn't laugh, but just looked at him with a puzzled expression on her face. "Virginia moon," she said absently, her voice low and distant.

"What's that?" he asked.

Carolina looked at him for a moment, feeling that trancelike state that she always did when their eyes met. "I— I don't know," she replied. "It's just...something sounded really familiar about the way you said that. About the moon in Virginia." She shook her head. "Just déjà vu, I guess," she concluded, but in her mind, she couldn't write it off so easily. This had happened to them before—one or the other of them had said something that had felt like a memory to her.

This can't be coincidence, she thought now. It had to be a sign that they truly were connected on a much deeper level.

"Yeah, something like that," Michael agreed, though he, too, felt as though more was at play here. Letting his gaze linger on Carolina for a moment, he felt a sort of tugging in the back of his mind, a sense that he had said those words before. Maybe it *was* just déjà vu, or a snippet of a long-forgotten conversation with somebody else. Either way, he had to let go of it—and get on with the matter at hand.

"Well, how about an island?" he suggested, turning in his seat a bit to face Carolina. At that, her face lit up.

"Yes, an island!" she agreed, placing her coffee cup back on the table. She pulled a leg up onto the chair in front of her, hugging her knee to her chest. In her mind, she pictured palm trees, sparkling blue water, warm breezes and coconuts and white sand. "A tropical island. That sounds *perfect.* What do you think, Michael? Does it sound good to you?"

Smiling at Carolina—he always seemed to be smiling at her; it was an involuntary reaction whenever he laid eyes on her—he reached over and ran a hand down her hair. He grasped the ends of it, savoring its silkiness against his skin. "Whatever will make you happy sounds good to me." He paused, letting her hair drop down again. "But what island? Where exactly should we go?"

Thinking about the question, Carolina took a sip of coffee, then gently sat her cup back down. She looked around again—an old habit; it still made her nervous to be so out in the open with Michael, even now when they were planning their future together—at all the people in their overcoats and jackets, brushing rain droplets off their shoulders and turning up their collars against the storm.

"How about this?" she said, turning back to Michael once more. "I have contacts in the travel industry. Why don't I talk to them, see what they think is good, and make a decision from there?"

Michael thought about it for a moment. "You mean...let you choose where we're going, and then take care of the arrangements?"

"Yes," Carolina replied, nodding her head. "That's exactly what I'm saying."

Raising his coffee cup in a sort of toasting motion, Michael grinned at her. "Bless you," he said. "The less legwork I have to do, I think, the better it will be for both of us. I'm hopeless when it comes to coordinating travel arrangements."

Carolina blushed a little, hugging her leg close to her again. "You trust me to make such an important decision for the both of us? I mean, this is where we could end up for—well, a very long time."

Reaching over to her again, Michael put a hand on her chin. "I trust you with my life, Carolina. I think I can trust you to buy us some plane tickets."

And with that, they both dissolved in laughter. Michael sat back again, feeling so relaxed, so at peace, so happy with his life—or, at least, with what his life was about to become. In a way, he couldn't believe that this was all really happening, that it was only a matter of time before he and Carolina would truly be alone together, as he had dreamt of so many times, as he knew they were meant to be. On the other hand, he couldn't see their lives unfolding any other way.

"Michael," Carolina said then softly, putting a hand on his arm, bringing him out of his thoughts. "Listen, we have to talk about something else, too—"

"What we're going to tell our spouses," he finished for her, knowing already what she was going to say.

"Yeah," she replied, looking down dejectedly. She hadn't really wanted to bring it up, had been trying to ignore the topic for the longest time, from the moment she'd agreed to run away with Michael. Somehow, though, she knew that their families had to figure into the equation; she and Michael couldn't just go away and leave them all hanging. They had to offer explanations, reassurances, something that might help them accept that—

"This is just how it has to be," Michael said, once again reading her mind. "Can't we just tell them that? It's fate, Carolina, we're powerless over it. We're doing what we have to do."

Looking over at him, Carolina didn't like how dark his face had grown, how upset he looked. She knew how torn he was about leaving his family, especially his children, behind. She wished that she could somehow make it easier for him.

But she also knew that such an explanation would not make anyone—themselves included—feel any better about it.

"You know we can't say that," she told him gently, intertwining her fingers with his, moving closer to him and talking softly. "We can't hurt them like that. I love you, and I know we are meant to be together forever, but if we say that to our families... Michael, they'll be devastated. And I know you don't want to hurt anyone if you don't have to."

Looking out the window again, his expression grew more serious than she'd ever seen it. His eyes scanned the street, following the cars and people as they passed, the wheels in his mind turning quickly. For a moment, Carolina was afraid that he would call the whole thing off, that in the face of having to confront his family—a seemingly insurmountable obstacle—he might back away from her.

However, when he began to hold on to her hand more and more tightly, she knew that he would do no such thing. Closing her eyes, she breathed out a sigh of relief, wondering how she ever could have doubted him.

"Here's what we'll do," he said at last, his eyes still on the street. "We'll just go." He paused, then looked at her again. "We'll go, Carolina. We'll get our plane tickets and get out of here during the day, when nobody's around. We'll leave them letters, but we won't mention one another. We can't. They can't know anything about us. About *us.* Not yet, anyway."

Letting the idea sink in for a moment, Carolina considered the logistics of it. She pictured herself seeing her kids off to school, her husband off to work—and then running to her bedroom, packing a suitcase, and jetting off with Michael, leaving nothing but a "Dear John" letter behind. Could she do it? Could she leave her family with such little explanation?

Looking at Michael, as usual, she knew that she could. With him, she could do anything, and this…this she simply had to do. Whether they could say it to anyone else or not, fate *had* brought them together, and they could not deny fate its due.

"Okay," she said. "Okay. I'll say I just need to get away for a while to sort some things out, and that I'll get in touch with them when I'm ready. How does that sound?"

Michael looked into her eyes for a moment, locking into her gaze and gaining strength from it. "It sounds good," he told her, knowing that it wasn't a perfect solution, but knowing, too, that it was the best choice they could make. "Good enough, anyway. At this point, what else can we do?"

***

Later that evening, the rain subsided and the temperature evened out. At home in her bedroom, Carolina opened a window just a little bit, letting some fresh air into the room.

"Long day?" David asked her. He was stretched out on his side of the bed, duvet bunched up at his feet. Reading glasses on, he held that morning's *Wall Street Journal* in his hands, his eyes heavy lidded and sleepy.

Slipping between the sheets, Carolina smiled at him wanly, unable to fully meet his gaze. She thought back on her afternoon with Michael, on the plans that they'd made and the long kiss he had given her before they'd parted.

"It's alright," he had told her again and again, holding her close, his lips against her ear. "It's alright, it's alright, it's alright."

"Uh, yeah, long day," she told David now, trying to sound lighthearted. "How was *your* day?"

Tossing the newspaper onto the nightstand next to him, David took off his glasses and rubbed his eyes. "Longest in history," he said. "Meeting after meeting after meeting. I always thought that being the head of a company would be a cakewalk. You know, long business lunches, golf games and schmoozing with other bigwigs." He looked over at her, smiling blearily. "But don't be fooled, Carolina. It really involves an awful lot of work."

She did look at him then, and smiled back at him. "You should take some time off," she told him kindly, gently, surprised by how exhausted he appeared. "You look like you need a vacation."

At that, he smiled brightly. "Hey, yeah!" he replied as he nestled down into the bed, pulling the duvet up over his legs. He turned back to her, rolling his head against the pillow. "Where should we go? Hey, how about an amusement park somewhere with the kids? We haven't had much quality time together lately. Don't you think that would be fun?"

Clearing her throat uncomfortably, Carolina shifted in the bed, lying down as well but slowly, her body tense. "Yeah," she agreed, forcing a brightness into her voice. "That sounds great, sweetheart."

David laughed. "Good," he said, his voice beginning to fade. Carolina could tell that he was already drifting off to sleep. "You get the plane tickets tomorrow. Let's go next week. I want to get out of here."

On her side of the bed, Carolina silently turned over to face the window, and a thin stream of cool air brushed across her face. She closed her eyes.

Next week, she thought. She'd already be gone with Michael by then. Michael, whom she'd been seeing behind her husband's back. Michael, for whom she was leaving her family. Michael...her soul mate, her fate, the man with whom she was forever meant to be.

It's alright, it's alright, it's alright, his voice echoed in her head.

"Goodnight, Carolina," David mumbled, and in moments he was already snoring.

"Goodnight, my love," she replied, but in her mind, she was saying it to Michael.

TWENTY-FOUR

Standing at the French doors leading out to the deck, Carolina stared out into the backyard. The sky was a dark, angry gray; large, heavy raindrops fell down from it at an amazing velocity, striking the ground with the force of a stampede of horses. The surface of the koi pond rippled and shuddered. The leaves of the Japanese maples quivered in the wind.

"Mommy, how do I look?"

Behind Carolina, Alexis' sweet, little-girl voice called out to her, and she turned around in response, her arms wrapped around one another for warmth. She drew her sweater a little further closed around her shoulders as she regarded her youngest child, almost thirteen years old now, decked out to brave the storm outside: pink raincoat, hood up; pink rubber boots with multicolored hearts printed all over them; a tall, cane-handled umbrella in her hand. With her backpack full of school books underneath the coat, she looked like a miniature hunchback. Carolina couldn't help laughing a little at her, and that made the young girl smile.

"You like it?" Alexis asked, doing a dramatic little curtsey.

Crouching down to her daughter's level, Carolina smiled warmly as she reached to adjust the raincoat's hood, to push it back a little. "You're beautiful," she said, then kissed Alexis' forehead. "You're growing into a really lovely young woman."

Alexis giggled. "Mom, I'm a girl, not a woman! I'm only twelve!" Then she skipped out of the kitchen in search of her older siblings.

Standing up straight again, Carolina wandered over to the kitchen table, where she had left her cell phone. Glancing at it—not picking it up; not wanting to rush things—she saw that it was 7:45. Just a few more minutes until everyone would be gone from the house. For a second, she let her mind wonder what Michael was doing, picture him in his own kitchen, talking to his own children...for what might have been the last time. But then, squeezing her eyes shut tightly, she erased that image from her mind.

Stay focused, she told herself. *Remember what you have to do here. Remember everything that happens.*

"Mom, do you have the car keys?" Patrick came bursting into the kitchen, his energy turned up to high, as usual. Carolina had always marveled at how her oldest child jumped out of bed in the morning, raring to go. He'd always been ambitious, always full of life. She'd admired that about him, but she wondered if she'd ever told him so.

"Uh, yes, I do," she replied, going over to her purse and retrieving them, then walking over to Patrick to hand them over. As she placed the keys in his hand, she reached up and smoothed back a stray lock of hair, then put her hand gently on his cheek. The light stubble along his jawline almost moved her to tears—her boy was becoming a man.

"I love you, baby, you know that," she told him, smiling and trying not to tear up.

Just as Alexis had, Patrick laughed at her words, though Carolina took no offense; they were children, after all, and had no idea what was really going on in her head.

"Mom, I'm almost eighteen," he said. "I'm not your baby anymore." He paused, though, and seeing the almost sad look on his mother's face, he relented. He gave her a quick peck on the cheek. "Okay, you can call me your baby, just make sure you don't do it in front of my friends, alright?"

Tossing the car keys up into the air a bit, Patrick caught them in his hand and then bolted out of the room again, calling to his sisters that it was time to get out of there. Rooted to the spot where she stood, Carolina simply listened as the rest of her clan came barreling down the hallway stairs and into the kitchen, the girls followed by their father as well. His spirit seemed just as high as the children's for some reason.

"Morning, sweetheart," he said, pecking Carolina on the cheek as he passed by her, en route to the coffee pot. He poured himself a cup and swallowed half of it in one shot, then let out a loud, satisfied sigh. "Now," he announced loudly, "I am ready to start my day!"

Briefcase in hand, trench coat thrown over his forearm, David came back and gave Carolina another swift kiss—a rarity that made her wonder just what had gotten into him.

"Have a good day, dear," she said faintly as he headed toward the door leading into the garage, patting each of their children on the head as he passed them. She raised her hand in a weak wave as he turned to close the door, and he smiled brightly at her.

As if nothing at all is different about today, Carolina thought. *As if all of our lives aren't about to change.*

And then, none the wiser, he was gone.

"Mom, are you okay?" Lindsay asked, standing at the table, stuffing books into her schoolbag.

"Yeah, honey, I'm fine," Carolina said. "Do you have money for lunch today?"

Pausing, Lindsay felt the pockets of her jeans, then her coat. Finding what she was looking for, she smiled. "Oh, yeah," she said. "I do."

"Good." Leaning back against the counter, Carolina regarded her sixteen-year-old, noticing not for the first time how much alike they looked. Lindsay had Carolina's same long, blond hair, her sparkling green eyes, her tall, thin frame. "Make sure you eat something that's good for you," she added. "Try to get some fruit, okay?"

Looking up at her as she hoisted her book bag onto her shoulder, Lindsay smiled. "I always do, Mom. You know I love fruit."

"Alright, girls, time to jet!" Patrick announced as he came back into the kitchen, straightening the collar of his coat. "In the car, in the car! Mom—" He gave her a crisp salute. "I shall see you this afternoon. Over and out."

Saluting him back limply, Carolina pursed her lips closed to fight back the tears once again. Letting her hand fall back to her side, she watched her troops lining up and marching toward the door.

"Love you, guys," she said to them.

"Love you, too!" they responded in unison. And then, they were out the door, and they, too, were gone.

Alone in the kitchen at last, Carolina bowed her head and let the tears come, filling the silence of the house with her sobs until she had nothing left.

And then she picked up her head and made herself keep going. She had a plan, and she had to see it through to its completion. It was the only way she could ever be with Michael.

As if on cue, her cell phone, still sitting on the table across the room, began to buzz and vibrate. Walking calmly over to it, Carolina put a hand up to her face and wiped away the tears that soaked her cheeks. Her eyes felt puffy and sore; she was sure she looked like a mess.

Flipping open her phone, she saw there was a new text message from Michael.

I'm ready, my love. Just waiting for you to come and get me.

Looking at the words, Carolina felt the pressure behind her eyes once again, but she refused to give in this time. Clearing her throat and shaking her hair back from her shoulders, she took a moment to clear her head, to get rid of the doubts that were threatening to overtake her.

Almost ready, too, she typed quickly. *Be there soon. Can't wait to be with you.*

Going to her purse again, Carolina dropped the cell phone into it and took out a plain white envelope, one that she had been carrying around with her for days. She hadn't thought it would be safe to leave it at home or even at her office, where someone might have seen it. She couldn't have risked letting anyone know about her and Michael's plan.

"David," the envelope said on the outside in red ink, in the small letters of Carolina's own handwriting. Opening it now to take one last look, to make sure that everything was in order, she took out the single sheet of paper it held and unfolded it. Standing by the table, one hand on the back of a chair to steady herself, she ran her eyes across the words written on the page:

Dear David,

I know this will come as a surprise to you, and I hope that you will understand, first and foremost, that the last thing I want to do is hurt you and the children. I love you all dearly; there is nothing more important to me in life than my family.

However, I have had a lot on my mind lately—things that I haven't talked to you about, things that I'm not sure you would truly understand. Things that I have to work out for myself.

So, that is what I am going to do. I am going to go away for a while—all alone, just to clear my head and try to sort things out. I don't want you to look for me. I will get in touch when I can to let you know that I am okay but, please, do not come after me. I will come back when the time is right, and when I am able to give you some more answers for all of this.

Please tell the children that I love them so much.

Carolina

Reading it now, she remembered the agonizing hours she had spent writing this letter, the many crumpled-up versions she had tossed into the trash can in her office. It had been so difficult to explain why she was leaving without revealing too much, without giving any clues about her relationship with Michael. Though she longed to be out in the open with all of it, she knew that this was not the right time for that.

Someday, she told herself, still looking down at the letter, her eyes lingering on the words that she wished could say so much more. *Someday soon.*

And then she put the paper back into the envelope and sealed it, and left it there for David on the table.

***

On the freeway, Carolina leaned forward in the driver's seat of her SUV, bringing her chest close to the steering wheel. Between the tears in her eyes and the still-raging storm outside, her visibility was next to nothing. She switched the windshield wipers onto their highest setting, hoping that it would help, but thinking that it probably would not.

"Get yourself together," she told herself quietly, dragging the heel of her palm underneath her eye to catch the tears that fell so freely to her cheeks. "This is what you want. This is what you want to do. What you are *meant* to do."

She sobbed again, almost uncontrollably, and gripped the steering wheel tighter. Her eyes welling with hot tears, she squinted them shut for a moment and then opened them.

"Oh, God!" she cried, her foot pressing hard on the brake pedal. Tires screeching, the SUV came to a slow, skidding halt mere inches from the car in front of it, which was stalled in traffic. All around her, horns blared and high beams flashed.

"Okay, okay!" she called back to them, even though she knew that no one could hear her. Sitting up straighter in her seat, she took a deep breath and blotted her eyes one last time with the sleeve of her jacket.

"You can do this, Carolina," she whispered to herself, looking intently out the front window, being sure now to keep a careful distance between her car and the vehicles in front of her. "You can do this. Think of Michael. Think of your life with him. Think of everything you have together."

And for the moment, those thoughts were able to comfort her. Instead of ruminating on the guilt she felt over leaving her family, she focused on the future and what fate might have had in store for her and Michael. She imagined how blissful it would feel to finally be able to be with him as she wanted to. As soon as they stepped off the plane, she thought, she would throw her arms around him and kiss him—and she wouldn't care who was there to see them.

Holding this image in her mind, Carolina felt more anxious than ever. She had to see Michael, had to touch him, had to hear him say that everything would be alright. Speeding up a little in the SUV, she began to weave in and out of traffic, winding her way toward the exit that would take her to his house. Rain be damned, she had to get there as fast as she could. Before something happened to make her change her mind.

Winding through the local streets, getting closer and closer to Michael, Carolina began to feel that old familiar pull toward him, the intimate, vibrational harmony that they shared. She'd experienced this with him before; they both had. It was just part of the phenomenon of their love, a sign that what existed between them truly transcended the plane on which they both lived. Somehow, as she turned the last corner onto his block, she knew that he would be standing outside waiting for her. In her mind, she could see his black suitcase, his soaking-wet coat, before she even pulled up to the curb where he stood.

Shoulders hunched, collar turned up against the wind, Michael grabbed his luggage and tossed it into the backseat of the SUV, and in a moment he was sitting next to Carolina. He shook out his dripping hair, brushed the chilly droplets off his sleeves and then rubbed his hands together, blowing on them to create a little warmth. When he was done with this routine, when he had adjusted to coming in out of the storm, he stopped, and he looked at Carolina as if it were the first time he was seeing her. They looked into one another's eyes for a long time, the trance overtaking them.

And then Michael reached a cold, damp hand over and touched Carolina's face. And then he smiled, and it lit up the car, the street, the whole city, as if the clouds had parted and the rain had suddenly ceased its campaign against them.

"Everything's alright," Carolina said. And in that moment, she knew that it was true.

TWENTY-FIVE

Lying on her back on a blanket, Carolina stared off down the beach. No one for miles; not a soul in sight. No cars, no airplanes, not even a boat far out on the water. The only sounds were the leaves of the nearby palm trees rustling in a slight wind, the gentle crash of the ocean's waves against the shore.

Turning her head the other way, Carolina looked at Michael lying next to her. He was on his stomach, eyes closed, head resting on one arm and turned away from her. He wore blue swim trunks and nothing else; some stray grains of sand clung here and there to his bare skin, which had grown so beautifully tanned in the three weeks they'd been on the island. They'd been spending every afternoon out there in the sun, enjoying the change in climate—in particular the lack of rain. Neither of them had looked so healthy in a very long time.

Carolina lifted a hand and brushed her knuckles along Michael's back, and his shoulder jerked slightly in response. She realized that he had been sleeping, and for a moment she felt bad for having disturbing him.

"Sorry," she said to him softly, turning over onto her stomach and putting an arm across his back. "Sorry, sweetheart. I thought you were awake."

Turning his face toward her, Michael was already smiling. He appeared so calm, so peaceful, so well rested, Carolina thought he looked like a whole new man, so different from the Michael she had known back in Seattle. This Michael was happy. This Michael wasn't stressed out. This Michael was free to be himself.

And to be mine, she thought, kissing his shoulder and then resting her cheek against it. *Mine, all mine, now and forever.*

"I wasn't sleeping," Michael told her then. "Just resting." He laughed a little. "Like we ever do anything else."

Laughing as well, Carolina pushed herself up to a sitting position, then stretched her legs out in front of her. "You say that like it's a bad thing."

Watching her adjust the top of her two-piece bathing suit, Michael paused. Though Carolina didn't really tan—she wore far too much sun block for any rays to ever get through—their time on the island had brought a lovely glow to her skin, a vitality that seemed to have been trapped within her when they'd been in the city. In a bikini, in a simple sundress, wearing nothing at all, she looked more beautiful, more radiant than ever. This retreat had done wonders for her in so many ways, Michael thought, reaching out a hand to touch her leg.

"There is not one bad thing happening here," he said.

"Isn't that the truth?" Carolina closed her eyes and turned her face up to the sun, smiling. "I haven't even answered a phone in three weeks." She thought for a moment. "Hell, I haven't even heard a phone ring."

Rolling over onto his side, Michael bent an arm and leaned his head against his hand. He looked up at Carolina, who ran her hands through her windblown, seawater-treated hair, messy and wild. He remembered how, a few days earlier, he had found a tree full of gorgeous, fragrant flowers, and had picked one and tucked it behind her ear. He remembered its soft pink petals, how they had brushed against her face. She'd looked so beautiful, Michael hadn't been able to keep his hands off of her.

In fact, he'd been having a hard time resisting her at all lately—and really saw no reason why he should even try to. Now that they were truly alone, they had all the freedom in the world to be together just however and whenever they pleased. There were no jobs to report to, no families to look after; there were simply no distractions of any kind. With nothing else on which to focus, Michael's and Carolina's senses were trained solely on one another, and a new power had developed between the two of them. Michael felt more drawn to her than ever, more attracted to both her body and her mind. And he knew that she felt the same about him.

"Well, what do you want to do this afternoon?" she asked him, picking her sunglasses up off the blanket and carefully putting them on.

Turning over onto his back, Michael put one arm behind his head and rested the other on his bare chest. He looked up into the clear, blue sky and considered the question. They'd spent a long, late morning in bed, as usual, talking about everything they could think of, laughing much and agreeing on just about everything. After lunch, they'd come out here to relax, as they did many afternoons; they would probably go for a long walk later as well, as was their habit once the sun began to fall lower in the sky. Strolling down the beach or into the jungle behind their bungalow, they would meander arm in arm, collecting seashells or flowers with which to adorn their temporary home.

And later on, in the middle of the night, as he often did, Michael would lead Carolina by the hand out to the beach and make love to her underneath millions of sparkling stars and the biggest, brightest moon they had ever seen.

But for now? "No idea," he said, squinting up at her, one eye tightly closed against the brightness of the sun. "You have anything in mind?"

Carolina looked over her shoulder, out toward the water. "I'm thinking about a boat ride," she said, nodding her chin toward an inlet a few hundred feet down the beach, where a small sailboat sat tethered to a dock. They'd taken it out several times since they'd been there already.

"Hey, that sounds good!" said Michael, suddenly sitting up. While brushing the sand off of his shoulders and arms, he looked out across the ocean. The clear-blue water was incredibly calm, barely any waves at all. "Looks just perfect out there."

Jumping up to his feet enthusiastically, looking forward to getting out onto the open sea, Michael held a hand out to Carolina. She grabbed it, and he pulled her up to stand beside him and then right into an embrace. He kissed her, slowly and gently, his hands pressing firmly against her back.

"You go get your sun hat," he said finally, letting go of her. "I'll go and untie the boat."

**

Adrift at sea with the love of my life, Carolina thought, reclining on the small, cushioned bench at the back of the sailboat, watching Michael. After adjusting the sail just so, he'd sat down beneath the mast, on the floor of the boat, toying with a compass he held in his hands. *No place else I'd rather be.*

"What's the direction, Captain?" she asked, and Michael lifted his face to look at her. He had his sunglasses on, although the sun didn't seem to be as bright as it had been when they'd left; that had only been an hour earlier, but already it seemed like late afternoon. For a moment, Carolina looked to the sky and wondered where all those magnificent rays had gone.

"North, I think," Michael replied, shaking the small, metal compass. He raised his eyebrows, a tentative smile on his face. "I'm not sure this old thing really works. I just found it in the toolbox under the bench there."

Carolina brought her feet up to rest on the edge of the boat. Leaning back onto her elbows, with her bright-blue bikini, floppy straw hat and big, round sunglasses, she looked like she was posing for the cover of a magazine.

"You look good like that," Michael told her, his gaze lingering on her. He reached up and took off his sunglasses so he could see her better.

Carolina's cheeks, already pink from the sun, blushed a deeper hue. She put a hand up to the top of her hat and threw her head back dramatically. She puckered her lips into a kiss. "How's this?" she asked, unable to keep herself from laughing.

Putting the compass down on the floor of the boat, Michael brought himself up onto his knees, then walked his way over to Carolina. Taking off her hat and gently placing it on the floor behind him, he ran his hands through her hair, setting it free in the light wind that blew across the boat and the sail. He took off her sunglasses as well and put them down inside the hat. Looking into her eyes for a moment, he felt a jolt of excitement course through his body.

"You're so beautiful," he told her quietly, somberly, and with one hand supporting her head, he kissed her, slowly and sweetly, in rhythm with the rocking of the boat.

"Michael," she said as he sat back again, this time nestling himself in next to the bench, leaning his back against it. Turning on her side, Carolina hung an arm down around his shoulder, her hand on his chest. "Do you…"

She didn't finish her question, but fell silent. Turning his head a bit to look at her, Michael saw that her face had grown pensive, even troubled. "What is it?" he asked, twisting his body to face her, worried about what had suddenly come over her.

Smiling wanly at him, Carolina looked away for a moment, out to the horizon. The water was rippling around them a bit; the breeze had grown a little bit cold. "I just," she began, but then stopped again. She had so much on her mind that she didn't know quite where to start. Finally, she looked back at him. "Do you think about home?" she asked plainly, relieved to finally have the question out there.

"Oh, Carolina," Michael said, shaking his head a little, the expression on his face full of sympathy. "Is that what you're thinking about?"

Nodding, Carolina pursed her lips and looked away from him again. She felt a little embarrassed now to have admitted it. There they were, together at last in this paradise, and she was thinking about what they'd left behind. This wasn't what she was supposed to be doing at all.

"Baby, don't worry," Michael told her, putting a hand on her chin and gently turning her face back to his. Raising his eyebrows, he looked steadily into her eyes, locking her in and keeping her gaze on his. "It's okay to think about that if you want to. I do too sometimes. I think we'd be inhuman if we didn't."

Carolina looked out over the sea again. "We left so much behind. We hurt those who love us. We've sacrificed everything." She looked back at Michael, her eyes imploring. "We will see our children again, and, one day, they'll understand. Our love is just so powerful, Michael. It's obviously taken control of us."

Nodding, Michael took her hand in his. "Carolina, do you think about our future together? I do... I think about us living together, maybe on this island, maybe somewhere else, maybe even back in Seattle. Who knows where we might end up, where fate might want to take us? All I know is that we will be together, now and forever. We will build a life together. That's what's meant to be. You are my future now, and my past, and everything in between. And no matter what else I think about, all thoughts will always lead me back to you."

Gazing into his eyes still, Carolina felt a warmth wash over her, a sensation of love and commitment and the thousand other emotions she felt every time she looked at Michael. "I love you so much," she told him, putting her hand on top of his. "I feel as though I've loved you for a hundred years."

"I love you, too," he told her. "More than anything and anyone." As he gazed deeply into her eyes again, that trancelike state overcame him, as it did every time. Michael was so compelled by her, by their past, their future, their eternal love. And he knew that Carolina felt the same way about him. Neither of them knew, however, just what connected—or reconnected—them both.

Noticing that the wind was beginning to turn the boat in a different direction, Michael stood up then and headed back toward the mast. "Better turn the sail a little," he said, reaching for the ropes that held the silk sheath in place.

"Sounds good to me," Carolina said a little absently, suddenly feeling a little bit tired. Laying her head back against the cushion of the bench, she closed her eyes and relaxed her body, letting it sway with the motion of the vessel. In the background, she heard Michael grunting as he pulled on the sail ropes, heard the clicking of the crank as he turned it to catch the breeze. The longer she lay there, though, the more muted these sound became, until eventually she drifted off to sleep.

***

"Carolina."

From what felt like a million miles away, she heard Michael calling to her, and the urgency in his cry brought her back into semi-consciousness. The air around her was cold; before her eyes even opened, her arms wrapped around her own body, rubbing away the goose flesh of her skin.

"Carolina! Help me!"

"Coming, Michael," she said softly, still half asleep, believing that she was hearing him in a dream. "Be right there, sweetheart." And then she turned over, and nearly fell off the bench on which she had been sleeping.

"Oh!" Carolina tumbled to the floor of the boat, awaking with a start. Grabbing on to the bench to steady herself, she looked around, confused about what was going on. The sky was almost pitch black, a cluster of thundering clouds approaching at a frightening pace. The sea had grown choppy. Its stilted waves pitched the boat this way and that.

"Carolina!" Michael called again, and she turned immediately toward the sound of his panic-stricken voice.

"Coming, coming!" she told him, scrambling to her feet, alarmed by the chaotic situation that seemed to be building up around her. In the distance, she saw a bolt of lightning hit the water. "Oh, my God! Michael, what's going on?"

At the main mast, Michael struggled to tether the sail down, but the wind worked against him. Anchoring himself with one foot against the edge of the boat, he held on to the rope with both hands, trying to rein the sail in.

"Carolina, help me," he repeated, and she grabbed on to the rope with him. Together they tried to steer the sail back in line with the rigging.

"Michael, what's happening here?" she called to him over the increasingly loud wind—and, now, the thunder. The sound of its rumbling caught Carolina's attention, made her whip her head around toward the back of the boat, where it seemed to be approaching.

"I don't know!" he shouted back, still trying as hard as he could to pull in the sail. "This storm just came up out of nowhere. I thought I could get the sail up and get us back to land before it reached us but it's moving at incredible speed."

"Yeah, I see that," Carolina answered, but her words were drowned out by another crack of lightning, another clap of thunder. The storm was growing closer by the second; heavy raindrops were beginning to fall. She put all of her weight on the rope, trying to reel it in, but as soon as the next gust of wind came, it slithered right out of her hands, leaving them burning.

"Michael, I lost the rope!" she shouted, but before she could hear his reply, the lightning flashed again, obliterating everything in whiteness. She felt herself flying through the air.

It hit the boat, she thought as she tumbled, her back hitting the mast and then the bench on which she had slept. "Michael!" she cried again, reaching out her arms, although she could no longer tell just where he was located.

"Carolina!" Michael called at the same time, his eyes recovering from the flash as the rope slowly slithered out of his hands. Looking up, he saw the scorch marks on the material of the sail, the crack in the wood of the mast. It had been hit, just as he'd feared. But that didn't matter now. All that mattered to him was finding Carolina.

"Where are you?" he shouted, ducking under the broken sail rigging, crouching to keep his center of gravity low in the tossing and turning boat. "Carolina!"

After making his way around the perimeter of the craft, Michael stopped once again by the mangled sail and looked out into the water, hoping against all hope that he would not find her out there.

And he didn't. Not during the first flash of lightning. Not during the second. But in the dark, dark water, when the third crack of lightning touched down only feet away from him, he saw his beloved Carolina floating in the ocean. And without a moment's hesitation, he jumped in and swam to her.

"Carolina!" he screamed as he reached her, trying to grab her in one arm while keeping himself afloat with the other. She was on her back, her wet hair plastered over her face. He brushed it away, making room for her to breathe.

"Carolina," he whimpered, tears falling freely from his eyes and into the vast expanse of the sea. "Carolina, don't leave me," he cried, putting his head down against hers, willing his mind not to imagine what his life would be like without her. They'd made so many plans together; they had so much to look forward to. They were soul mates, meant to be together. It just couldn't end like this. As kind as fate had been to bring them together, it couldn't be so cruel as to tear them apart.

"Not like this," Michael whispered as he clung to her, as the waves lapped over them, threatening to pull them both under.

And then, in the eye of the storm, despite the thunder and the lightning and the wind, Michael heard the sweetest sound he could have imagined.

"I'm here," Carolina said weakly, her eyes still closed. "Michael, don't let go of me."

"Never, never!" he cried in reply, covering her face with kisses and wrapping both arms around her body. "I'll never let you go. And if by chance we lose each other, I will always find you again."